The Kaye Berreano Mystery Series, Book 1: Safe Beginnings

By Christine Duncan

Writers Exchange E-Publishing

http://www.writers-exchange.com

The Kaye Berreano Mystery Series, Book 1: Safe Beginnings
Copyright 2018, 2025 Christine Duncan
Writers Exchange E-Publishing
PO Box 372
ATHERTON QLD 4883

Cover Art by: Sandy Cummins and Jatin

Published by Writers Exchange E-Publishing
http://www.writers-exchange.com

Contents

Dedication

To Jerry with all my Love
And of course, to Millie.

Chapter 1

I turned the V. W. into the parking lot of the battered women's shelter, where I worked night shift. An icy wind rocked the car, typical for January in Denver. The weatherman predicted snow, if you believed him. I didn't. It felt too cold.

I heard the crunch of gravel under my tires as I pulled in. Then I caught sight of my soon to be ex-Volvo in the headlights. Roger sat in it alone.

What brought him here? He got out as I parked, and stood staring intently into my headlights. He looked suave in the same gray suit and topcoat he'd worn that afternoon for our session with the lawyers. His short dark hair stayed neatly combed despite the weather.

I took my time getting out of the car. I resisted the urge to smooth my own always-unruly, dark hair. No way I'd primp for him. But I belted my red woolen coat around me like armor, knowing how it flattered my olive skin. Then I methodically gathered my purse and papers together, trying to think why he'd come. He was supposed to be spending his time on Monday nights with our daughter, Hannah. Was something wrong with her?

I saw him smile at me, his teeth white and straight. No, he wanted to charm me into something. Still, I couldn't help worrying. "Where's Hannah?" I asked. "Is there a problem?"

He shook his head. "I dropped her off at a friend of hers on Alkire Street. She'll be home by curfew. I wanted to talk to you alone, without any lawyers."

Oh, right. "I've got to get to work." Nothing he could say would interest me, especially after that preliminary divorce hearing today.

"It's ten to, Kaye. You've got time to hear me out."

I shrugged and leaned against the VW, wishing I still smoked so that I could pretend coolness by lighting up. He and I had quit together a couple of years back.

"Look, if it's about me changing my name back to Berreano, I've already...."

"It's about the whole thing." He stared down at me, trying to look sincere. "I think we'd work things out better ourselves," he said. "I've read where couples can save thousands of dollars by arranging things to suit themselves. Let's leave the lawyers out of it. They only complicate things."

Thousands of dollars. Wouldn't his lawyer, Arthur Patterson, be thrilled to hear that? "I thought you liked Art."

He smiled that phony smile he used on clients that I hated so much. "I've been thinking about what you said about the car."

"Um hmm," I made my voice non-committal.

"You said," he looked at me as though he was a good little boy who had learned his whole lesson, "You needed a new car and new furniture."

"Roger, you know this. The way you've structured the agreement, you get everything, including the house, and all the furniture. It was pulling teeth to get you to give me the little bit of money you did. I had barely enough for a down payment on the house I bought. And there you sit with ten times that amount stashed away in the bank. You tried to make me feel lucky to get the kids' bedroom sets and the TV from the family room. I sleep on a camping cot, for heaven's sake."

"You ought to feel right at home--or should I say work?"

It took me a minute to realize he referred to the rollaway cot they kept at the battered women's shelter--an amenity I've never used. "Great, Roger. Just swell. Another slam at my job." He'd never liked my job from the day I took it over two years ago.

To hear him tell it, he'd never even contemplated an affair until I worked nights. I felt that after twenty years of marriage, he should be able to put up with a few nights without me.

"It's a wonder the kids see you at all. I'm going to put custody on the table here too."

I started to leave, but he grabbed my arm.

He looked at me, his face serious. "Look, I'm sorry. I shouldn't have said that. I'm really here to try to settle things."

"Yeah, what?"

Roger shrugged. "The settlement...you know, everything."

"The settlement. What settlement? Have you heard anything I've said? Everything is yours. All you gave me were the mismatched linens. Why should you get the good car too, when I'm the one who will never have the money to replace the old one?"

"Hey, you made this decision here. You were the one who wanted this divorce."

"What did you want--a ménage a trois? I'm not moving in with Bambi."

"Brenna." He held his hand out to stop me. "That's water under the bridge. I'm trying to compromise with you here. Now hear me out."

I closed my open mouth and glared, arms folded over my chest. No way I'd want anything he wanted to give me, but I'd give him five minutes.

"As I said, I thought about you needing furniture. Why don't you take the stuff in the family room? You've always liked it."

True. In that whole miserable professionally decorated house, the family room was the only real place to relax. Roger and I bought the furniture together. The serene blues and sand colors of the room reflected the colors of the beach I grew up near back East. The room's casual, laid-back feel would look wonderful in my new house. No more lounging on floor pillows. And if I didn't have to spend money on furniture, maybe I could afford a good second-hand car soon.

"I've decided to redecorate anyway."

He would redecorate for that bimbo and expect me to be happy with the castoffs?

I forced myself to look off somewhere else for a moment trying to master my anger. The cold crept into my bones, and I shook with it and my rage, equal parts. I heard the crunch of heels on the gravel.

Amanda Gannon, a tall athletic blonde, came around the side of the safe house and waved, then got into her red Neon. Normally we had a curfew for residents, but Amanda worked a night job at a factory manufacturing kidney dialysis equipment, so we made an exception for her--in more ways than one. Most of our residents were victims of abuse. But a judge, known throughout the Denver area for his quirky sentencing, remanded Amanda here for beating up her husband, George. She claimed self-defense--but I didn't see any bruises on her. George ended up in the emergency room. I waved back, but I couldn't make myself look happy. Luckily, she didn't appear to be feeling chatty either. The red taillights of her car disappeared out of the driveway before I could make myself respond to Roger.

I drew myself up to my full five foot two, but I made my voice smooth, though I felt like gritting my teeth. "Sure, I'll take the furniture."

Roger put that fake smile on again, talking to me through it, giving the impression of a puppet with an immovable jaw. "That's great. Then it's settled. I'll talk to Patterson tomorrow, let him know. "

I held my hand up, trying to act calm. "But I want the Volvo too."

"Too? Yeah right, Kaye." Mister calm-and-collected's voice was rising. His smile looked more like clenched teeth. "That's not the deal."

"That's the deal I want."

"Listen, I'm not going to stand here while you try to take advantage," he shouted.

"Fine. Don't." I smiled now, as I hadn't been able to smile at Amanda just moments earlier; a heady, I've-won-this-one smile. I walked away with the satisfying conviction that I'd pricked Roger's sugary shell. At least I felt satisfied until I saw a cluster of women at the red curtained window of the brick bungalow, watching their night counselor have a fight with her estranged husband. Then like a balloon the day after the party, all the air came rushing out.

The kitchen felt warm after the chill outside. I closed the door slowly. The women had moved from the window to gather around the red Formica and chrome table, talking. The shelter had used the table long enough for it to develop retro-chic, like the rest of the room. I hated retro-chic. I would have loved to remodel the whole room, from its glass fronted birch cabinets down to its rounded top refrigerator. If we only had the money.

Right about then it felt as though the room was filled to bursting with every resident in the house. When I really looked, there were only three of them. They stopped talking abruptly. Somehow, I faced them, making myself look every single woman in the eye.

They applauded.

Mary Ellen sat with her hands primly in her lap on one end of the table. In the middle, Nicky, Mary Ellen's young and pregnant roommate stretched her long, jegging covered legs. Closest to me lounged Barbara Washburn, wearing red sweats that warmed her cocoa skin, but did nothing for her short chubby figure.

"Look, guys, I'm sorry you had to see that." I felt my face getting hot with embarrassment.

"Way to go, Kaye," said Barbara, dunking a cookie in her mug, then raising the mug towards me in salute.

"Really. We have to show these SOBs what's what," said Nicky, her tiny, pointed face smiling. She looked tired. Harried as I felt, I noticed that. Tired, but proud of me. She swung her legs to the ground and got up to get another pop from the stash she kept in the fridge. She didn't even appear pregnant from the back.

Even Mary Ellen nodded and smiled, although I knew that her religion didn't believe in divorce. Dressed in a beige double-knit shirtdress, with her long mousy hair escaping from its tight braid, she looked like a caricature of the bookkeeper she was.

Embarrassed, I shook my head and headed for the office, hoping for some time alone to calm down. Unfortunately, the sleeping porch office was already occupied. My boss, Liz Windfield, looked up from her gray steel desk calmly. The woman had her shoulder cried on at least a couple of times a day. Her eyes narrowed in concern, as she pushed the sleeves of her soft plum sweater up to her elbows. She said, "Want to tell me about it?"

I didn't. I shook my head and made a business of taking my coat off so I didn't have to look at her. "Personal problems," I said.

She shrugged her sturdy shoulders and nodded as though she'd expected that answer, and proceeded to update me on the day's changes. Nicky had found an apartment and hoped to move in about a week. Cindy had a lead on a job, but seemed afraid to take it since the man who wanted to hire her knew her husband well.

We had a possible new one coming in. A shelter in L. A. had a woman trying to get away from a Crips gang member, and she could arrive that night or the next.

I frowned. "That's pretty dumb. The Crips have people here in Denver too."

Liz said, "If it's a problem, we'll pass her on to somewhere else."

I nodded. We'd done this kind of thing before, acting as a sort of underground for women who got involved with guys in gangs or organized crime.

I sighed, took Liz's notes and told her goodbye.

Most of the women settled down early. I had a few sporadic crisis calls. One woman wanted to know if slapping constituted abuse. When I assured her it did, she got quiet and got off the phone quickly. The house stayed peaceful except for the barely heard thump of a bass coming from someone's boom box. I took the time to catch up on some of the reading on counseling that I needed to do.

The phone rang again. "Beginnings, Battered Women's Shelter."

"What a crock. Ain't no battered women there," he whispered.

I leaned forward as though that would help me hear, but the only word I could make out next was dykes.

"Can I help you?" I knew I sounded irritated.

He laughed. "I'm gonna help you, Honey. Get all those ladies out of there and send them home to their husbands where they belong before it's too late."

"Too late for what?"

"That's all I'm gonna say. You just make sure you listen." With a click, he was gone.

Harassing phone calls were part of the routine, but we tried to be careful about them. You never knew. I called security, who promised to get with the phone company and the police. I also noted it in my shift log. In other words, I did what I could to make sure everything was all right. But I still felt unnerved. Glancing out the window across from my desk, I even thought I saw something move outside. I stood up so quickly, I almost toppled the rickety office chair. I pressed my nose to the window. Snow swirled against the cold glass pane. The fenced back yard was empty.

I was letting this get to me. I needed to think about something else for a minute and calm down. I looked at my watch--nine o'clock. I decided to call home to see if Hannah made it in. She might be fifteen, but she thought she was an adult and should not be subject to curfew. My hand was on the phone almost before I completed the thought.

"Hello?" RJ dropped his voice an octave, trying to sound older, I guess. Mostly he sounded out of breath.

I heard Hannah say loudly enough to compete with the music in the background, "Oh yes, RJ, you jerk. Give me the phone."

"Don't fight, kids," I said automatically, for what good it did.

He dropped the phone, and I heard them scuffling and breathing hard. Just when I was wondering if I should call someone in to work to cover for me so I could go home, RJ shouted, "Hannah, you dork, it's Mom."

Then the heavy breathing stopped, and the music volume went way down. RJ came back on the line.

"What in the name of all that's wonderful is going on?" I asked, gritting my teeth so I wouldn't yell.

"Nothing," he said in that innocent voice that would have tipped me right off, even if I hadn't heard the scuffle. Right now it was play, but Hannah wouldn't take much before she got mad.

"RJ? Hannah does not have to have your permission to be on the phone."

"She's been on the phone all night with Josh. I'm sick of it."

"All night? I thought she just got home."

A heavy sigh came over the wire. "She's been on the phone ever since," he said.

"RJ, you leave the phone alone. Do I have to call your father to go over there and baby-sit you two?"

"What? No."

I'd never threatened that one before, and RJ definitely didn't like it. I filed that away for future reference. Not that I was likely to carry it out, considering Roger's attitude toward my job.

"Then leave the phone and your sister alone."

"I will."

His promise seemed genuine. I decided to take him at face value. "So except for this, how's it going?"

"Fine."

"Did you lock both doors?"

"Yes, Mom, we locked the doors."

"Got your homework done?"

"I'm working on it."

"How about Hannah? Is her homework done?"

"She's doing hers, too."

I could tell from his long-suffering voice as I questioned him that he wished he had let Hannah have the phone. He kept it perfectly polite, but he sounded bored.

"All right, I'll stop nagging you," I said. "But you behave."

"I always do, don't I?"

"I love you, RJ. Tell Hannah I said goodnight."

I missed the cheerful noise of home as soon as I put the receiver back on the cradle. The phone seemed to be dead after that. I felt restless, and uneasy.

At two-thirty I heard a knock, and went to let Amanda in, her work shift done. She didn't speak, just waved a tired hand and took herself upstairs. She'd probably gone straight to bed. I wished I could do the same.

Not long after that, I heard noises in the back hall. Perhaps I was wrong. Sometimes Amanda headed to the kitchen after her work shift for a little snack before she went to sleep. It must be her. I got up and stretched cramped legs as I walked down the hall. The kitchen was dark. All I heard was the hum of the refrigerator. The noise I'd heard must have been the heater or the house settling or something.

I went back to the office and flopped down in the battered desk chair, wrapping the neon afghan around me. The house felt chilly and empty, and it was one of those nights when I wondered if Roger wasn't right about this job.

It must have been close to three when I heard a loud buzzing noise. I jumped up, flung the afghan back on the chair and raced into the hall before my conscious mind realized that the blaring mechanical drone was the fire alarm.

Smoke billowed from Mary Ellen and Nicky's room. I had to get everyone out.

"Mary Ellen! Nicky!" I roared out their names, pounding on their door with my fists. Smoke seeped out from underneath. I'd had enough training to know that I should leave it closed.

Oh, God, now what? I'd forgotten the fire extinguisher. Should I run back and get it? Thick dark smoke dimmed the hall light above me. No, first the fire department.

I couldn't handle this by myself. Our alarm would alert our security company, but I couldn't wait for them to call to confirm before they turned it into the fire department. The women and kids inside that room didn't have that long.

I ran back to the office and dialed 911. "It's Beginnings. I mean, this is Beginnings Battered Women's shelter."

"Yes ma'am," said the unruffled voice of the operator. "And you are?"

"Kaye Atchinson--Berreano, I'm the counselor. We've got a fire."

"We're on our way, Ma'am."

"Hurry." I banged the phone down then ran up the stairs for the rest of the women. I raced from room to room, thumping on doors, yelling over the screech of the upstairs alarms which were just starting. "Come on. Everyone out. Now. This isn't a fire drill."

The stairwell acted as a conduit, so the smoke already clouded the upstairs hall. Doors began to open, and a chorus of buzzes filled the air as individual bedroom smoke alarms responded. Shrieking dark figures stumbled for the stairs, some shepherding smaller crying shapes.

I followed close behind them. "Come on. Come on, hurry." Smoke caught in my throat, making my voice hoarse, but I tried to sound calm and authoritative.

I watched the last woman disappear down the murky stairs then inspected each room to make sure that everyone in the upper part of the house was out. Then I returned to the downstairs bedroom.

The door was still closed and the hall was, if possible, smokier than before. Oh dear Lord, why didn't either of these women wake up? Nicky had two kids as well as her unborn baby. It wouldn't take much of this kind of smoke to kill them.

I had to get them out. I ran to the bathroom and got a towel, wet it and tied it mask like around my face. Then taking a deep breath, I went in. Heat and smoke hit me in the face. My eyes teared about the makeshift mask. I couldn't see anything except the fire below the window.

Smoke billowed toward me, powered by the air from the open window. As I watched, the air from the open door fanned the flames to the ceiling. I felt the heat scorching me from here. Fear filled me. I had to get out of there. I had to get these people out of there.

"Nicky! Mary Ellen!" I screamed as I started feeling around blindly. Nothing but clothes on the floor. Thank God. I'd had pictures in my mind of children collapsed by the door. I felt around some more.

I heard the crackling of the flames as I searched. Why didn't the alarm go off in here? The bottom beds were empty--which meant Nicky's kids got out. Maybe they'd all escaped. I stood on a lower bunk and felt around one of the upper bunks one more time to make sure.

No. Someone lay still in the bed.

I felt around, since I couldn't see. Too slender to be Nicky's pregnant body.

"Mary Ellen," I screamed in her ear, and shook her. This had to be more than just a deep sleep. I grabbed her shoulders and tried to drag her out of her bed. "Unh," I grunted as I heaved as hard as I could. More tears stung my eyes. The upper half of her body moved with me, but her legs still lay tangled in the bed sheets. She dangled awkwardly from my arms. How could someone so thin be so heavy?

Where happened to the fire department? What was taking so long? I stood for a moment with Mary Ellen in my arms, screaming and crying. "God, what is going on? Mary Ellen, wake up. Help me, I can't do this alone." I shook her again and almost lost my grip on her. My knees buckled under her weight. I had to do something. Sweat ran down into my eyes, and I coughed uncontrollably through my makeshift towel-mask.

"Help!" I yelled through the smoke. The snapping, popping sound of the fire was the only response I heard.

Chapter 2

No one responded to my screaming. Alone in a burning house with an unconscious woman, I stood there, trying to pull myself together. "I can do it. I know I can." I whispered the encouragement to myself under my breath. I cleared my throat and said more loudly, trying to convince myself. "If I drag her, she's going to get hurt. Hurt? She's going to die. I have to get her out of here." I pulled hard on her shoulders. Mary Ellen's lower body hit the worn flowered carpet with a thump.

Dragging her was no easier. I marked our inching progress on the squares around the carpet roses. It couldn't have taken as long as it seemed, but I was afraid to look up and see the flames by the window. The fire crackled loudly, and the heat seared the uncovered part of my face and hands. The smoke was now so thick, I couldn't stop coughing.

Mary Ellen wasn't coughing. A bad sign. I leaned over and screamed in her ear. "Mary Ellen, for God's sakes, wake up! You have to wake up." I should have saved my breath. Sweating and hacking so hard I wanted to puke, I pulled her out of the room. Then I stepped back over her to shut the bedroom door in hope of containing the fire. Sirens shrieked in front of the house. Trembling and crying, I bellowed, "Help! We're in here." Mary Ellen still didn't stir.

Boots clomped heavily towards us. At the same time, I heard voices at the back of the house. Someone shouted, "Get that hose over here." Almost immediately, I heard the sound of water spraying the door in front of us, hitting it hard.

Three firefighters in breathing apparatus appeared. My throat was so sore and congested, I couldn't say anything.

One of the firefighters nodded toward us then turned and ran up the stairs. The short one gestured toward the front door. They wanted me out. I nodded at no one in particular and struggled to move on quaking legs. I felt him take my arm and I leaned gratefully on him. As we labored down the hall, I looked over my shoulder to see the third firefighter kneel next to Mary Ellen.

"Thank God, you guys are here. What took so long?" My voice was hoarse and breathy. The short fireman raised his eyebrows at me through his mask. Could he talk through all that stuff? I wondered. It didn't stop me from babbling on. "Mary Ellen's going to be all right, isn't she?" I didn't stop to see his response. "I'd better let someone know what's going on. I've got to call my boss."

I tried to turn toward the office and the phone, but the fireman's arm tightened and he steered me firmly toward the front door. He looked at me as though I were a little kid caught drawing on the walls in the restroom at school.

"I'm leaving," I said, keeping my eyes on what I could see of his face under the breathing apparatus.

He opened the door and followed me out. Then he shut the door firmly behind both of us.

The clean night air made my throat clog up, and I coughed hard.

He pulled his mask off, and I could see that he looked barely old enough to be out of school. "You need to see the paramedics," he said. "Let them check you out."

What paramedics? I wanted to find the residents and make sure they were all right. I needed to call Liz. My breath hung out in front of me in the cold night air. It felt like such an effort to lift one foot after the other, and I couldn't stop shaking. I shivered, wrapped my arms tightly around myself for warmth and looked around.

Two fire trucks, an ambulance and two police cars all stood out front, all with blazing lights. The engines hummed loudly. None of the women were here.

"I have to call my boss," I rasped. "I have to let her know what happened. This is a shelter for battered women, you know."

Mouth tight, he took me by the arm again and led me toward one of the trucks. He reached into the cab and pulled out a cell phone. "Make it short," he said. "This is for official business only."

I turned my back to him and dialed Liz's number with trembling fingers.

"What happened, Kaye?" Her voice, always husky, verged on scratchy and faded; telling me how tired she was. By now it was going on four in the morning. "How bad is the fire?"

I'd forgotten security would have informed her when the fire alarm went off. "I don't know." I coughed and tried to catch my breath. "I think it's just the downstairs bedroom."

"Good. Good." I could almost see her nodding. "Anyone hurt?"

"It was Mary Ellen Schuster's room. She's unconscious."

I heard Liz suck in her breath on the other end of the line, and then silence. I thought the phone went dead, but no such luck.

"What about Nicky and her kids?"

"I don't know, I think they got out." A spasm of coughing shook me. I struggled to continue, my voice rough. "I tried to drag Mary Ellen out, but I couldn't get her very far. What's going to happen, Liz?"

"First we need to make sure everyone is all right. Then if the house is still habitable...?" She made it a question.

"Definitely."

"Then how...?"

I knew what she meant. If it were such a minor fire, then how did Mary Ellen wind up in such bad shape? Another fit of coughing hit me.

The fireman tapped me on the shoulder. "You need to wind this up." He extended his hand around me as though to take the phone from me. "You need to see the paramedics."

"Okay. I'm going," I said, over my shoulder.

"Are you still in the house?" Liz's voice was shrill in my ear.

"No, no, I'm outside. I guess I'd better go get looked at. I'll call you as soon as I know what's going on."

"My God, yes, get yourself checked out right away."

I handed the phone back to the young fireman, who stashed it back in the truck. "So where are my residents?" I asked him.

"Where you should be--with the paramedics," he said, with a hint of barely restrained impatience.

He took me by the arm and guided me down the drive toward the parking lot.

It was mass confusion down there. A rescue truck, its light strobing over the parking lot, stood in the middle of the lot. Several women lay on stretchers next to oxygen tanks. A rescue worker bent over a child I dimly recognized as Aleia Pfeiffer. She cried uncontrollably, her chubby eight-year-old-body shivering, although a blanket covered her. Starr Pfeiffer hovered, sobbing.

The other women huddled around the parking lot talking in high-pitched voices. A head count showed nine women and eight kids all present and accounted for--all, except Mary Ellen, of course. I couldn't let myself think about her right now.

"Hey," said my fireman. "I've got another one for you." He nudged me forward, watched to see the paramedic nod, and shot back up the drive.

Women dressed in an assortment of nightclothes and sweat suits crowded around me. Many faces sported little mustaches from the smoke. Cindy Arbitus spoke first. "What happened, Kaye?"

I started hacking so hard my eyes watered. I shook my head. Someone shoved a cup of water into my hand and I drank, noticing distractedly as I did how grimy my hands were. When I could talk, I said, "It looks like a small fire, in the downstairs bedroom. I'm glad to see you and the kids got out, Nicky."

She looked confused. "Yeah well, you practically pushed us out the door."

It was my turn to be confused. When had I pushed her? I didn't even see her leave.

"Mom, I'm tired," whined Bud, Nicky's three-year-old. She bent down and picked him up awkwardly, hefting him over the bulk of her stomach. Her eighteen-month-old daughter, tufts of baby blonde hair still tousled from her crib, reached up with both arms to be held too.

My eyes stung. I thought she and those kids were dead for sure. With her short dark hair standing on end emphasizing her small face and large eyes, she didn't look much older than my Hannah did. She was so young and she already had two little ones and another on the way. Her life was already hard enough. Did she have to go through this, too?

The EMT left Aleia and came over to me. "Are you having any trouble breathing, Ma'am?"

"No, no. I'm fine," I said, unable to take my eyes from the scene around me.

"Why don't you come over here a minute and let us check you out?" He led me over to the oxygen tanks. I sank gratefully down on the blanketed ground and let him take my heart and pulse rate. But my mind was racing so fast, I couldn't concentrate on his questions. He offered me a blanket, and I huddled under it appreciatively.

Finally he said, "I want you to sit here for a while. I'm going to give you an oxygen mask to help you breathe."

"I don't want one." It sounded childish, and I hoped he wouldn't ask why, because I couldn't give him a reason.

He looked at me appraisingly. "You sure? It will help you clear that smoke out a little quicker."

I shook my head. "No, I don't want one, please."

"All right. You just sit there a bit."

I nodded, and he moved back toward Aleia and Starr.

The snow started to get serious, collecting on the hair of the women clustered around me. I needed to decide if I should call another safe house for temporary shelter or if I should concentrate on getting everyone back in the house.

Even as I was thinking that, a bus drove up into the parking lot with a Red Cross logo on the side.

One of the rescue workers with the oxygen tanks said, "We put a call out for a task force. We need some place for you all to get warm."

"Can't we go back into Beginnings?"

"They have to assess the safety of the structure, Ma'am. It all takes time."

I nodded, distracted. Someone in the front of the house shouted and I strained to hear. "Is there a counselor or somebody in charge, back there?" I looked up at yet another EMT.

"I'm the counselor." I tried to signal him by waving my arm.

He must not have seen me because he strode out of sight.

I stood up, shedding the blanket.

"Take it easy now. You've had a shock," The nice paramedic objected.

"I'm okay," I said, waving him off. My legs full of pins and needles, I hobbled back up the driveway, and squinted, looking carefully at the house. I didn't see any damage. Why couldn't we go back in?

As I rounded the corner of the house, I saw Mary Ellen. She lay still on a stretcher with a mask over her face as they loaded her into the ambulance. I crossed the yard at a half-run, ignoring my prickly legs.

"Is she going to be okay?"

The tall blond EMT shrugged. "She's alive. We need to transport pretty quick, but I'd like to get some information, if I can. You the counselor?"

"Yes. I've got all her information on file in the house." I indicated the open door. "If they'll let me go in, I can..."

He shook his head. "Just tell me what you can." He bent over a clipboard. "Name?"

"Mary Ellen Schuster."

"Address?"

"I don't remember. Somewhere over by First and University, I think."

"Any relatives we should notify?"

"She's got a husband, Harry."

"Phone number?"

"I don't know. I mean not off hand." I felt so helpless. She'd just gotten here the day before. I did her intake interview too. So why couldn't I remember? "If I could just go in..."

He shook his blond head again. "You know her medical history, prescriptions, anything that can help us here?"

Now I shook my head, "She didn't mention any medicines. I know I asked. It's a standard question."

The City of Denver posted signs all over that cars would be ticketed and towed if parked on the snow emergency routes during a storm. No one but tourists, and I suppose Roger, took the chance of parking there and getting stuck. This had been an unusually snowy January, and the forecast for Monday night had been for six inches or more of snow.

"Did you call my... Roger?"

"I wanted to talk to you first. You didn't use the car that night?"

"The Volvo? No." My laugh sounded bitter.

"Do you know if your husband was around the safe house that night?"

"Tuesday?" I stalled clumsily. I needed time to think.

"Monday." Wiloski's dry tone told me he was aware of my delaying tactic. Oh what the heck. "He came down to talk to me."

"What time was that?"

"Around nine."

"Did he say anything about what he planned on doing after that?"

He wouldn't have any plans for a Monday night except bed, probably, with that bimbo he was seeing now. But not even she would be allowed to disturb the eight hours sleep Roger felt were essential for him to do his job at Laurel, Thomas, and Atchinson, Public Accountants. That was how he ended up a partner. "No."

Officer Wiloski cleared his throat, which came out as a loud rasp on the phone line. "How is your relationship with your husband going, Kaye?"

It appeared Wiloski knew how to stonewall too. I knew this information had to be on record from our talk the night of the fire. "We're getting divorced."

"I noticed your name was different from what was on the car's paperwork. Had to call around to see who Katherine Atchinson was."

What did this have to do with my marriage or divorce anyway? Did he mean...? "Roger doesn't have anything to do with what happened there that night."

Why I defended him, I'll never know. Roger was a jerk.

"Just checking out everything," Wiloski said cheerfully.

"Should I get the car?"

"Your husband picked it up after the incident. But I'd like a chance to talk to him about this."

Naturally, he'd picked it up. He'd had it at the courthouse in Golden yesterday. I dialed Roger's number right away. All I got for my pains was his answering machine. It gave me some gratification to know that he'd have to listen through my hang up.

This was not like Roger. He liked staying home. He never let the machine answer for him either. If he were home, even if he were in the john, he'd answer.

Yesterday was Thursday. Had Roger picked up RJ for visitation?

I went to RJ's room, hoping to be able to talk in a conversational tone, but I still had to shout. "RJ?"

No answer so I barged in and waved toward the stereo.

He wrinkled his nose at me. But he unfolded his tall, skinny frame from his pretzel position on top of the metal frame bunk bed, leaped over a pile of dirty clothes, and turned it down.

"It wasn't that loud, Mom."

Maybe the hearing loss was already permanent, and he really just couldn't tell anymore. I shook my head at him. "I didn't come in here to talk about that, although I have to tell you my blood pressure just went down about twenty points."

He scowled, probably anticipating the rest of the lecture which would center around his ragged black jeans.

I decided to forgo the preliminary skirmishes this time and get down to business. "How did it go at your Dad's last night?"

RJ dug his toes into the pile of clothes, which seemed to require all his attention just then. His black sneakered feet turned the pile completely over like a farmer turns compost before he answered. "He called yesterday and said he couldn't make it."

"Did he say why?"

RJ shook his head, still staring at the clothes. "It's not like it was important or anything."

"It is if it bothers you."

"We weren't going to do anything, Mom. It was just..."

"You were looking forward to it."

He nodded. "He wouldn't have missed on Hannah's night."

"What?"

He finally looked up at me, and I felt surprised to see tears winked back in his blue eyes. "This is the second time he's missed on my night."

Yes, I remembered sometime around Thanksgiving, I think it was; Roger had missed on RJ's night, but only because he had gotten a terrible case of the flu. "Honey, he was sick."

"He wasn't sick on Hannah's night."

"So what? You think he got sick just because it was your night?" I shook my head. "Look RJ, your father loves you just as much as he loves Hannah. The divorce doesn't change that at all. If he couldn't come last night, there's a reason, I know, and he'll make it up to you later. Just like he did when he had the flu."

I meant it. Roger might be a scuzball as a husband, but the kids meant the earth to him. He had come up with some great seats at a Nuggets game last time, and I knew he wouldn't miss another night unless he had to.

RJ just shook his head again, looking back down at the rug.

God! Why hadn't Roger explained whatever the problem was? Didn't he know how this affected the kid? RJ wasn't going to believe anything I told him now. I hugged him. "You'll see," I said.

I stood watching him a minute, but he didn't look up. Reluctantly, I left, resolving to talk to his father about it.

When Roger did get around to explaining, I wanted to hear the explanation myself-- about this, and about the night of the fire. Roger had never liked my job at the safehouse.

* * *

"You're just the person to represent the safe house for the funeral, tomorrow," said Liz when I got to work that night.

"Why is that?" I asked, as I tried to take off my coat without taking my eyes off her.

"For one thing," she said, "none of the other counselors got a chance to know Mary Ellen."

I started to say something, but she wasn't finished. "And of course," she said, beaming, "you are short on hours right now, so this will give you a chance to put a few more hours on your time card."

There was that. "I won't have to go to the wake, will I?" I didn't do wakes even for money.

"You mean the visitation? That's tonight, and I believe it's private. All you have to do is go to the service and convey our condolences to the family. Oh, and try to make arrangements to return Mary Ellen's belongings."

The night went slowly and I felt exhausted by the time I trudged out of the safe house that evening under dark snowy skies. I cursed myself for not wearing water-proof shoes. My feet were freezing wet by the time I hit the car, but I felt more miserable inside.

The talk had repeated the same theme I'd heard before. No one liked Mary Ellen. At one point I started to wonder if one of the other residents started the fire to scare her away and inadvertently killed her. It seemed unlikely. But I'd seen people do some pretty weird stuff when they're under stress. And no matter how we counselors tried, being in a shelter for battered women was stressful.

We'd had one woman--a very quiet, soft-spoken type--who had sneaked out of work to vandalize her husband's car. On successive days, she had slashed his tires, spread some gummy stuff on the front seat so that when he sat down his clothes would be ruined, and finally stuck some sugar in his gas tank. We found out when the cops came around to question her. And that was just one example of how some of these women reacted to the stress of the safe house and their battering.

Yet I couldn't really believe one of these women killed Mary Ellen. But what about her husband? What about my husband for that matter?

My cold car felt as tired as I did, not wanting to start in the fifteen-degree temperature. I switched on the wipers, hoping to get out of scraping, but no such luck. I lumbered back out of the car, gloveless of course, to do a slapdash job of it. I ran through suspects with each stroke of the scraper: Nicky, Mary Ellen's husband, my husband.

Roger couldn't have. After all, why would he? Sure he hated my job, but that was all over now. He had a girlfriend. But even if Roger didn't, whoever did do this was still out there somewhere. It could be anyone with a grudge against the shelter or, as Liz had pointed out, the Crips may have gotten word we had someone they were after.

I got back in the car. The heater put out cold air that left the windshield frosted on the inside and the steering wheel still icy under my reddened hands. It occurred to me that it was Friday. Mo had been using her vacation time to take Fridays off since she got pregnant. I could call over there. I needed to talk.

RJ lay spread out in front of the TV when I got home. His warm black coat and sneakers had been discarded in front of the front door where I tripped over them.

I steadied myself on his black shirted shoulder and he didn't even look up. I glanced at the TV to see what was so engrossing. One of those sci-fi shows--the kind with the alien sightings. Music blared from Hannah's room.

"Hannah doesn't have a date tonight?"

RJ shrugged, still watching the TV. "I think she ditched Josh. She's all mad."

Josh had seemed a little boring to me, but I'd never have said so to Hannah. Whenever Hannah was between boyfriends the whole family suffered. "Great." I sighed. "Besides that, did everything go okay tonight?"

"I guess so. Mom, I'm trying to hear this."

"All right. Look, I'm going to give Mo a call. Could you turn it down?"

RJ glared but complied.

Running quickly downstairs, I banged on Hannah's door to get her to do the same. Then back upstairs, still wearing my coat, I called Mo.

"Hey!" She sounded a little revved.

"I was going to apologize for calling at eleven-thirty on your night off but it sounds like you were up," I said.

"I was. No point in going off schedule just for the weekend."

I knew what she meant. Mo's shift over at Denver General was from three to eleven. She and I had discussed before how drained we could get trying to keep the same hours as the rest of the world on weekends and going back on swing shift during the week. "I need to talk," I said.

"Come on over."

"You sure? What about Bill?"

"No problem. He's playing with his computer."

That was all I needed to hear. I went back through the living room where RJ looked half asleep. A commercial for some telephone girlie thing was on. Oh the joy of late night local T.V.

"Show over?"

"I guess."

"I'm going over to Mo's. Hopefully, I'll be back before too long."

"Mo's?" His whole face lit up. Maureen spoiled both the kids, and they adored her for it. "Can I come too?"

I almost said no, but what the heck, they didn't have school the next day. "You'll have to vanish while I talk to Mo."

"No problem. Bill got a new scanner for his computer, and I've been dying to mess with it."

"Bill's already on the computer."

"Great. Maybe he'll show me some stuff."

Don't ask me what there was to mess with about Bill's new scanner. To me, a computer was something to work with, but RJ loved the things. I sighed. Something else I should really be providing for him. Roger already had one, naturally.

In the end, Hannah decided she'd come too, bundling her slender body into RJ's discarded black peacoat. I didn't care; at least the coat covered over that skintight pink tee she knew I hated.

RJ, however, took offense, and glared heavily.

She opened her blue eyes wide, trying to look innocent I think, and flipped her long blonde ponytail over the collar of the coat. "What?"

He drew his hand up sharply, indicating the coat.

"You don't like it anyway. You said it made you look like a preppy." She made a face at him, mimicking his tightly pursed mouth as though daring him to dispute what she said.

He tightened his mouth even more at that, but said nothing, disappearing into his room for a hooded sweatshirt, which he probably got off the floor. They had been squabbling too much lately.

Maybe Roger was right. I needed to spend more time with them. I decided to ask Liz for a shift change. If I worked daytimes, I'd be with them more.

Both kids were mercifully quiet in the car, dreaming about computers, I guess. I drove to Mo's slowly, my thin tires not reacting well on the snowy streets. As I drove, I half-heartedly listened to the weather. The temperature had been dropping all day, and the weatherman droned on about what we could expect for stock show weather. Old-timers in Colorado liked to scare newcomers with tales of stock show blizzards and cold.

I'd noticed other years though, that the weather during the annual stock show was just annoyingly typical. If we were having a bad, snowy winter, then it would be the same when the end-of-January show came around. If it were a nice, warm winter, the stock show was warm too.

Still, to hear this weatherman tell it, stock show weather was invariably miserable, and any storm coming in now was sure to be a blizzard. I switched my windshield wipers on faster and squinted a jaundiced eye at the white-out conditions through my windshield. This time, he looked to be right. The worst part was the safe house could expect an upsurge in crisis calls afterwards. Cabin fever, like Christmas, made some guys mean. And we were in no position to be taking on new residents.

Maureen and Bill rented half a duplex in Northwest Lakewood, another suburb of Denver. They'd been kicking around the idea of buying a house, which, considering the good salaries they both made, seemed pretty sensible. If they were going to do it before the baby, I personally felt they were leaving it too late.

Mo opened the door, the big black shadows under her eyes belying the smile on her face. The baby had gotten so big that her blue, babydoll maternity top looked stretched to the limit. Her freckled Irish complexion seemed paler than usual. Her long mahogany hair, bundled carelessly up in back, lacked its usual shine.

She waddled slowly across the room in front of us. So much for the radiance of pregnancy--I felt tired just looking at her. She waved us after her into the long living-dining room, chatting carelessly with Hannah about her shoes.

RJ sat at the glass table in her dining area, shrugging his coat off onto the back of the chair. From the little, all-white kitchen leading off the dining area, came the gurgling sound of a coffee pot.

The house appeared as neat as it always did, and the thick beige carpet looked freshly vacuumed. The African violets that Mo loved were in bloom on the marble window sills and overflowing onto a metal plant stand. A Dieffenbachia in a basket in the corner of the room, sported a bow. I wondered vaguely if I'd missed Bill and Mo's anniversary, but no, wasn't that June? I turned my attention back to my niece.

"I swear, Maureen, I think that baby's dropped."

She groaned. "Don't start. I've still got almost a month till my due date, and I want to work right up till the day."

"Well, at least if you go into labor at work, they'll know what to do."

Bill's stocky figure came out of the study. His eyes looked red-rimmed and swollen, as though he were tired--or had been staring at the computer too long. His short dark hair looked mussed. I looked back at Mo speculatively. Maybe they were fighting?

"Huh." Bill snorted, as he did some hand-slapping greeting with RJ.

I hoped they wouldn't fight while we were here. I'd better keep the topic away from her job. That was probably it. He didn't like her hours at all.

Mo nodded at me. "Get you some coffee?" She was already moving toward the little kitchen.

I stood up again. "Yeah, but let me. You sit down."

She wrinkled her nose at me. "You and Hannah both treat me as though I'm going to break. I'm pregnant, you know, not sick."

Hannah peered out from under her blonde bangs and steered Mo toward one of the dining chairs, standing over her until Mo sat down. "Well, you look both," she announced.

What could I say? She'd inherited my tact.

I felt pretty much at home in Mo's kitchen since the kids and I had stayed with them before we bought our house. It didn't take long to assemble some cups, napkins and dessert plates. Hannah helped bus them all out to the dining table while I checked the oven for the cake I could smell baking.

We all sat around the big glass table munching on hot apple coffeecake with vanilla ice cream. The coffee tasted as strong as I could hope for. I took a long, hot sip and burned my mouth in the process Bill, RJ and Hannah talked computers, and Mo and I caught up on some of the family gossip. I relaxed as I hadn't been able to in days.

Bill didn't say much to me or Mo, but I could see he was tired. I resolved to drag the kids out of here the moment the dishes were done. This had been just too selfish of me.

Of course I knew Bill and the kids would disappear into the den, leaving Mo and I with the cleanup--and time to talk about what was bothering me.

Thank God for dishwashers.

"So what is going on at the safe house?" Mo asked as she scrubbed at apple goo inside her oven.

"We're still at the Red Cross shelter."

"That's something."

I must have looked at her strangely, because she explained, "If the fire department really thought there was some danger still present, they would have made you disband."

"Yeah, I guess." I rearranged some glasses on the top shelf of the dishwasher, trying to cram a few more in. "Liz and some of the women in the shelter are afraid the Crips did it."

"Why's that?"

"Some woman from L. A. was supposed to come to us that night."

"It doesn't sound like their style," Mo said. "Wouldn't they do a drive-by shooting or something?"

I grunted my agreement. "I just don't think she was the target, though."

"Mary Ellen? What's your alternative?"

"Just half the world. Anybody with a grudge against the safe house... my husband..."

"Whoa!" Mo had been heading for the sink, but she stopped to turn around and stare. "Why would Roger...?"

"I don't know." I pushed the top tray of dishwasher in, rearranging the bottom now. All I had to do was get two more plates in. "He was there that night. We were arguing about the settlement, you know?"

I looked up to see Mo nod, then hurriedly looked back down. I didn't know why but I felt like crying, and if I looked at her for one more second, I would have. "Anyway, next thing I know the cops call. The Volvo's been towed from a snow emergency route. Was I the one who got it?"

"Did you?"

"If I had gotten that car, would I be driving the V. W.?"

"So where'd they find the Volvo?"

"By the safehouse, and they didn't tow it until the wee hours of Tuesday morning."

"Sooo." Mo let the air out slowly. "But why would Roger...?"

"He never liked the safe house. You know that."

"He didn't like your hours; he felt that it was hard on your marriage."

The same argument Mo had with Bill, I knew. But what could she do? She needed to work. I hadn't had to during my marriage to Roger, financially at least. Roger didn't want me to work period. And he hated the idea of it being there. It felt so shoddy to him.

"Still, he would never start a fire..."

"I never thought he'd cheat on me either," I burst out, letting the tears go.

Mo got a tissue box off the counter, and handed it to me, her hands dripping from the sink. "I know. Kaye, I'm sorry. But still, cheating on someone and burning down a shelter full of battered women isn't even in the same ballpark."

"He never picked RJ up Thursday night."

"Did he say why?"

I shook my head, then wiped the tears off my face, lowering my voice so the kids wouldn't hear. I didn't want them to come in and see me crying either. They'd had enough emotional upset over the last few months. "RJ was crushed."

"Poor kid," Mo finished scrubbing the cake pan and put it up on the dish rack. "Still, you don't seriously think that Roger would do something like try to burn down the safe house? There must be someone else."

"Like I said, half the earth. Nobody liked Mary Ellen. The whole safe house is glad she's dead. I'm to the point where I suspect everyone including the minister who brought her in."

"Really?" Mo said.

"No--not really. At least not the minister." I threw the tissues away and looked under the sink for the dishwasher soap.

Mo's voice sounded muffled. "I would."

I must have heard that wrong. I withdrew my head from the cabinet to hear better. "Huh?"

"If he's the same one we had in the hospital that night, he's just nuts enough to do it. I guess Mary Ellen's mother called him in. You could hear him all over the emergency room, ranting and raving."

"Short, bony guy, dark hair, gray at the temples?" I asked.

"That's the one. The guy has problems. He said the fire was a judgement on Mary Ellen 'cause she should have known better. Women should know their places, don't you know?" Mo raised an eyebrow.

I laughed. "You can't be serious," I said.

"Oh yes. Then he talked about how Mary Ellen should never have left her husband, and about how Jesus promises it will be better to die than to lead just one of His little ones astray. He made it pretty clear he thought the safe house had led Mary Ellen way off, and Jesus wouldn't like that. No one should interfere with a marriage, and there were special punishments in hell to those who do. The guy's a fanatic. He'd be first on my list of suspects."

Chapter 8

I hate funerals. No surprise; everyone hates funerals, right? But knowing something like that about myself did make me wonder why in heaven's name I'd agreed to come to Mary Ellen's. I wanted nothing more than to go back home, be with my kids and have some chocolate. A lot of chocolate. I sighed. To cheer myself up, I let myself wonder if the fire investigator would come too. What was his name? Farrell.

My fingers felt stiff from the cold outside as I signed the guest book. The weather had stayed perfectly rotten. We'd accumulated six inches of snow during the night, and the wind whipped it around enough that some drifts were twice that. Driving had been miserable. Of course the weather was supposed to be awful for funerals, wasn't that the rule?

The church itself looked cute, one of those little storybook types, white with the big steeple. Apparently they believed in cutting heating costs during the week, because the little tiled entry felt too cold to let my hands thaw out.

As a consequence, my writing, which needed to be clear so the family could tell that I'd been here, came out in a thin black scrawl.

I felt a tap on my back and turned around to see Amanda looking uncharacteristically solemn in a black knit dress, her coat slung over her arm. "Hi, what are you doing here?" I asked.

She shrugged and twirled around to include a short, slight, fair-haired man in a dark blue suit. "Didn't I tell you? Mary Ellen and I go way back. This is George's church."

"Really?" That explained a bit. I'd wondered where Mary Ellen had heard of the safe house.

"Let me introduce myself," said the fair-haired man reaching out a hand to shake mine. "My wife thinks I know everyone that she does. I'm George Gannon."

"Hi. I'm Kaye Berreano. I'm a counselor at Beginnings."

George looked exactly as I had imagined he would from Amanda and Dina's description. He stood at least two inches shorter than Amanda and was smaller boned. I would have bet money, if I had any, that he ran a couple of miles every morning. He looked the type. He had an easy-going, boyish face. He looked too laid back to know how to cope with Amanda's combination of fire and energy, especially when she got angry.

"Kaye," he tapped his cheek with his forefinger thoughtfully, "Amanda's told me about you."

There was a swell of music from the organ.

"We'd better get seated." He gestured toward the red-cushioned wooden pews in front of us. "Would you like to sit with us?"

"Thanks." I nodded, avoiding looking at the flower-covered white casket beyond the pews

We crowded into a pew with two older ladies, at once two men and a small squat woman, all of them dressed in black, marched past us to the front pew, right behind the casket.

"That's the family," Amanda said in a whisper that could have been heard back in the shelter.

"Which one is the husband?" I tried to be quieter.

A small woman in a smart black suit with white details, who was standing in front of us, heard me. She twisted around and pointed at the tall man with thinning dark hair. "That's her husband, Harry. I think the other is Mary Ellen's brother."

I nodded. It made sense. The shorter one appeared to be a masculine copy of Mary Ellen with the same, small-boned, mousy look. Harry was good looking, despite the receding hairline, with high cheekbones and a moustache.

"He looks like a real lady killer," I said, before I realized the words coming out of my mouth.

Luckily the woman in front of me didn't catch the pun. "Harry? He thinks he is." She nodded. "He's got 'em on a string at work. I told Mary Ellen." She nodded again.

"So you work with Harry?" I asked.

"Um hmm. Well, I work in accounting. He's in sales. I'm Olivia Springer." She reached back to shake my hand.

"I'm Kaye Berreano. I knew Mary Ellen only for a short time--I've never met her husband."

The organ music swelled again. With a friendly nod, Olivia turned back to the front of the church. Reverend Honecker, whom I recognized from the night he brought Mary Ellen to Beginnings, stepped up to the pulpit. He was dressed in a cheap black suit.

The music swelled and then cut off abruptly. Honecker started to speak. To tell the truth, I blocked out most of the good reverend's sermon--right after the part about all are sinners. I could tell right then what kind of sermon it would be.

I didn't like the guy anyway. He'd irritated me the first night I met him. I don't know why. He was just a scrawny, little man, with dark hair graying into wings around his ears. The biggest thing about him was his smirk. I couldn't stand to listen to him. I spent the balance of the funeral blocking out his loud meandering monologue and wondering who killed poor Mary Ellen. It didn't matter that she'd gotten off on the wrong foot with people at the safe house. This funeral, the coffin that I didn't want to look at, the grieving relatives--it brought it all home. No matter what she did, Mary Ellen didn't deserve to die. And since it couldn't have been an accident...

"Someone in this room could be called home to the Father this very day. Are you right with the Lord?" Honecker's voice boomed into my thoughts.

That reminded me about what Mo had told me the night before. Still, he'd have to be a real zealot to try to burn the safe house down in the name of Jesus, wouldn't he? Nicky had more motive than that--or the Crips. Or Roger. Or handsome Harry.

So he had all the ladies at work on a string, did he? I wanted to know a little more about that.

Honecker's ranting tones finally died away. I came back to the present to hear the organ drown the shuffle of the pallbearers' feet and the sobs of Mary Ellen's burly mother. The congregation murmured as it got ready to leave. I tapped Olivia on the shoulder. "Are you going on to the cemetery?" I asked.

She wrinkled her nose. "No, I don't think so."

"Me neither. You want to go have coffee?"

She raised a well-groomed eyebrow. "Sure, why not? But I'd like to pay my respects to the family if I could."

I nodded. "Me too."

I waved at Amanda and George who were busy talking to the old ladies on the other side of them, and slipped out of the pew.

One thing strange about this funeral--they hadn't set up a time for the grieving relatives to greet their guests. We caught up with the family outside the church where a moving van for a house across the street blocked the passage for the hearse and the family's limousine. Mary Ellen's mother stared stoically out at the street as her son stared at his black-clad toes on the cold concrete. Harry stood a little apart from the two.

Olivia walked up behind Harry and touched his black coat lightly to get his attention. I trailed behind. He turned with a smile and took her hands in his. I felt Mary Ellen's family watching. "Olivia, how nice of you to come."

"Harry, I'm so sorry," she said. She turned and they both looked at me.

"Mr. Schuster, I'm Kaye Berreano from Beginnings." I glanced sideways at Olivia, hoping I wasn't giving away any family secrets but not knowing how else to identify myself to the grieving husband.

Olivia didn't even blink, so I couldn't tell if she'd heard of Beginnings before or not.

Harry's eyes narrowed. His face took on a wary look. Was that because he was afraid of what Mary Ellen might have said about him?

Mary Ellen's brother stepped back as if I was contagious. But her mother closed in on me as soon as she heard the name, and I felt surrounded, which was absolutely ridiculous. Mary Ellen's mother was so short she barely came up to my shoulder. But she looked solidly built, her gray hair molded ruthlessly into a helmet-like hairdo. The expression on her face left me in no doubt that although she had never seen me before in her life, she didn't like me. "What are you doing here?" she said in an East Coast accent.

I backed away a little as she came closer and closer. "I wanted to convey my sympathy, and the sympathy of all of us at Beginnings," I said.

Olivia watched, eyes wide, avidly taking it all in. I could almost see her inwardly licking her lips.

"We don't want sympathy from you," said Mary Ellen's mother.

Harry's light gray eyes flicked back and forth between his mother-in-law and me. As though making up his mind about something, he smiled, and extended his hand. "You'll have to excuse my mother-in-law," he said. "She's naturally upset today. Aren't you, Ethel?" He cast a solicitous look at his mother-in-law that I wouldn't have believed for a second, if I were her.

Apparently, we thought alike. Ethel glared at Harry. "Don't you even talk to me, you..."

Luckily, Rev. Honecker chose this moment to break in, putting an attentive arm around Ethel's shoulders. "Mrs. Milford," he said. "This is too much to expect of you, when you've already been through so much today."

I wondered whether he referred to the delay of the hearse, or my intrusion on the scene.

Then Honecker cast a nasty look at Harry, so I decided that let me off the hook. "Why don't you come inside now and wait?" he asked.

Seeing my chance to deliver Mary Ellen's belongings go down the tube, I decided I'd better seize the moment. "Before I let you go, Ma'am," I said, "there are some things of Mary Ellen's I need to give you."

Her face told me what she thought I could do with the stuff, when I had a sudden inspiration. "Unless of course, you'd rather I gave them to Mr. Schuster."

That decided the matter. "You can bring them over to my place after church tomorrow," she snapped. "Charles can give you directions."

Obviously, Ethel Milford wanted her son-in-law to have nothing whatsoever of Mary Ellen's. With Honecker's arm still wrapped around her shoulders, Ethel swung around to the church and disappeared back inside.

"So who is Charles?" I murmured.

Harry heard me and smiled. "My brother-in-law," he said. "Should I introduce you?"

But Charles, who had been hanging back from the scene with his mother, had apparently heard. He came forward hurriedly, his mouth pursed. I couldn't decide who he found more distasteful, Harry or me, but Charles acted polite. "It's really easy to get to," he said. "But if you'd like, I'll draw you a map."

I had the map in hand and was moving away when I bumped into Amanda and George again.

"Oh, Kaye, there you are," said Amanda breathlessly.

"What can I do for you?" I said absently, still looking at the directions to Ethel's.

Amanda hesitated long enough to make me glance up and catch her looking at George as though she wanted him to say something. He saw us both staring and cleared his throat, jerking his head to ask me to move away from the funeral crowd. Curious now, I moved with them, out of earshot from the congregation.

"We were just wondering if you were still going to meet with us today?" George said.

Oh yes, their counseling appointment. My God, I'd forgotten. "Of course, I will."

"Great." Amanda grabbed George's arm, and they were starting to move away before I thought to question. "If you don't mind my asking, what went wrong with your counseling with Dina?"

George's fair skin blushed easily. He looked hot despite the cold weather. "The thing is, things weren't working out that well with Dina."

"What precisely was the problem?" I asked.

Amanda shrugged and looked at George.

He turned even redder and then blurted, "How do you expect some bull dyke like Dina to understand about the kind of relationship between a man and a woman?"

"I beg your pardon?" I knew my tone was icy.

Amanda put a gloved hand on George's arm. "I'm sorry, Kaye. George is such a redneck. But he can't get that idea about Dina out of his head, and he can't talk to her."

Jerk. I shook my head and started to walk away.

"Kaye, please," Amanda said.

I turned around, my mouth a tight line. "As it happens, Dina had already sensed there was something wrong with the counseling, although I hope neither one of you said this to her."

"I never did," said Amanda. George shook his head.

"Fine. So I will take over for her, but I want to set you straight. I won't tolerate any bigotry. If you don't like homosexuals, blacks, Jews, or women, keep it to yourself."

George nodded, his face scarlet now.

"And," I softened my voice. "To the best of my knowledge, Dina is not gay. She is married, she has a baby, and she's one of the nicest people I know; so if you have any problems with her, I don't want to hear them."

He nodded again.

"Fine. So we said we'd meet at two?"

Amanda and George exchanged glances and nodded.

I shrugged. Roger took both kids on Saturdays. "Okay. Then two it is, at Gunther Toody's?" I named a restaurant nearby that they had used for these meetings. It seemed a pretty poor alternative to private counseling, but with the fire and the need to keep the shelter's location secret, there was no alternative but a public place. According to the police reports, George hadn't been the violent one, but still we had a need to ensure the client's and the therapist's safety.

Amanda nodded this time and the two left before I could change my mind.

When I returned to the funeral crowd, I found Olivia waiting. I wondered just exactly what she had witnessed. She'd hung on through both scenes like a hungry dog hangs over the empty bowl.

"I'm sorry," I said, not knowing if I was apologizing for George, or Ethel, or the length of time Olivia had had to wait for me.

She waved a careless arm. "No problem. I understand. Your car or mine?"

My V. W was acting up as much as Mary Ellen's mother today. "If you don't mind, I know of a coffee shop down the street."

The coffee shop was one of those upscale places with marble tables and uncomfortable little chairs, where they charge an exorbitant fee for a cup of European-style coffee. To me, that meant coffee strong enough to melt the spoon. Since I tended to like my coffee so weak I could see the bottom of the cup when it was full, I liked to avoid those places. My pocketbook couldn't stomach them either. Still, Olivia looked pleased as she ordered an espresso and took a table under a long, weepy-looking fern.

She sighed happily, inhaled the coffee smell and took a long drink.

I explored the contents of my cup more cautiously. Anything this black had to taste like the stuff you scraped off the bottom of burnt pots. I'd rather have a cup of good old American truck-stop coffee anytime. What I'd really wanted was a big thick piece of chocolate.

I stopped mid-sip when she asked, "What is Beginnings?"

If I'd had any more in my mouth, I would have spit it out in surprise. My own mind had been pre-occupied with how to lead up to the questions I wanted to ask her, and I'd already forgotten that I had mentioned Beginnings in front of her.

"It's an agency for the betterment of women," I answered, making it up as I went along. Mary Ellen had a right to privacy, and I cursed myself for not thinking of another way to identify myself to her family without tipping off any bystanders. "Mary Ellen had only recently gotten involved with us."

Olivia raised her eyebrows. "Her mother certainly didn't seem to approve."

I twisted my mouth ruefully. "No, she didn't, did she?" I sipped at my coffee, eyeing Olivia. This woman didn't miss much, which would be great when it came to getting information about Harry from her, but first I had to figure how to swing the conversation that way.

"Is this the same place where Amanda is staying?" Olivia asked.

I stared. How could I answer that?

Olivia waved a small, pampered hand, her pink, perfectly oval fingernails a foil for her soft, white skin. "Oh, don't worry. I know Amanda. She's never been the type to keep secrets. She told me herself that she's living at some battered women's shelter because she beat up George. It's kind of ironic if you ask me."

I smiled and nodded, taking refuge in my dark bitter coffee. I watched Olivia carefully over the cup. This woman was obviously a world class gossip, much more skilled at extracting information than I could ever hope to be. Maybe I should cut my losses and run before I said something I shouldn't. I put the coffee cup down and reached for my purse.

"But Mary Ellen is a different story." Olivia leaned over the table, her large brown eyes serious. "Amanda can take care of herself. Always could. And so can George, if he's pushed to it. But Mary Ellen didn't deserve any of this. Harry ought to be taken out and shot."

"Why do you say that?"

Olivia leaned back in her chair. "Why it's perfectly obvious, isn't it? Or am I jumping to conclusions here? He beat Mary Ellen, didn't he?"

Uh oh, here we go again. I got up to go. "I'm sorry, Olivia. I can't tell you anything about Mary Ellen's situation..."

"As well as cheating on her?" she continued. "You think he killed her, don't you?"

She had caught my lady killer comment. I should have known.

"I don't know much about Mary Ellen and her husband. And what I do know, I'm not at liberty to divulge." I smiled, ready to say my good-byes and walk away.

"But the news said there's a question about that fire at the safe house, isn't there?"

If I answered yes, wasn't I acknowledging that Mary Ellen had been there? I stayed silent, purse in hand.

Olivia waved her hand again. "Don't worry," she said. "I know about how these things work. Don't say a word." She sipped at her coffee, tapped the cup thoughtfully, then said, "What do you want to know?"

Maybe she did understand. I sat back down, but on the edge of the flimsy little chair, prepared to leave if things got out of hand again. "Are you sure that Harry was cheating on Mary Ellen?"

"My dear, it was common knowledge for years."

"Where? At the office? Did Mary Ellen know it?"

"If she didn't, she would have had to be blind as well as deaf and dumb. He slept with anything in skirts."

"Yes, but sometimes guys like that want to be married to protect themselves from the other women," I said, almost to myself.

Olivia nodded and glanced at me shrewdly. "You must have known a man or two like that yourself."

I flushed, thinking of Roger. Was he really that way or was my bitterness leading me to think that way now?

Olivia went on. "That was Harry to a tee until he met this last one. This one he wants to marry. And Mary Ellen wouldn't give him a divorce."

"How could she refuse? All he had to do was find a lawyer."

"Something to do with money. Or maybe it was the house?" Olivia pondered, tapping her index finger against her lips, eyes scrunched shut. "I can't quite remember," she said, eyes popping open. "The details must have been vague. But it must have been financial. She had no children to hold over him."

Maybe it was just rumor. Maybe he was unfaithful, but Mary Ellen never said a word about divorce. "How do you know all this?"

"She told me, of course. The girlfriend did, I mean. She's quite desperate--which I would be too, if I were pregnant, young and in love with a married man. Would you like to meet her?"

Chapter 9

I didn't have a lot of time to think about Olivia's revelations, let alone meet Harry's girlfriend. I had to get to my next appointment.

My next stop looked a lot homier than the coffee shop by Mary Ellen's church. Gunther Toody's based itself on a fifties diner theme: black and white checkerboard floors, waitresses in starchy aqua uniforms and jukeboxes playing oldies music. Loud oldies music--so loud, in fact, I wondered why Dina had ever met here with Amanda and George.

Amanda and George were both waiting for me in a vinyl booth toward the back, wearing jeans and matching Texas Aggie sweatshirts. They waved me back so cheerfully no one would ever know they'd attended a funeral earlier in the day, or that they were here for marriage and anger counseling.

"I've never been here before," I said as I settled in the booth opposite. "Whatever made Dina pick this place?"

Amanda shrugged. "I picked it," she said. "I like it here. It's cheerful. Besides, it's about half way for both of us to come."

I nodded, shouting over Elvis singing about a hound dog, "Okay. I'm not sure that this is someplace that I would like to continue meeting, but we can talk about that later."

A middle-aged waitress with a chest full of buttons that said things like "My job is secure, no one else wants it", came up to take our order.

After the espresso place, I was leery of coffee. This was my chance to finally have the chocolate I'd been waiting for all day. But now that I could have it, I didn't crave it. "I'll take a strawberry milkshake."

"Okay, Hon." She nodded, her improbably blond ponytail bobbing.

George ordered for himself and Amanda, but at the last moment, Amanda added coffee shooting a defiant look at her husband.

George, fair skin shining in the restaurant's bright lights, shook his head at her as the waitress walked away, a long, lacy white slip showing at the back. "Now you know you shouldn't have that, Amanda Jean," he said.

"Why not?" I asked. "Does caffeine give you a headache?"

"Shoot no," she said. "It's just that George's church says you shouldn't have coffee 'cause it's a stimulant."

"I see. How do you feel about that?"

"If I want coffee then I'm gonna order coffee, church or no church," Amanda said, her face stony. She avoided looking at George.

Apparently, I'd stumbled on an old argument. "Okay. Let's backtrack a minute here. I've read the file that Dina kept on you two, but since I wasn't involved with your counseling, other than talking with you a little, Amanda," I nodded at her, "I don't really have a sense of where you are going. Have you established some goals for these counseling sessions?"

George snorted. "Shit, yes." He flushed. "Sorry. I didn't mean..."

"I should hope not," said Amanda, glowing with triumph. "Isn't cursing a sin in that church of yours too?"

"Now don't you go rubbing it in." George looked at me as he explained. "Sometimes I slip back into my old sin ways, but with the grace of Jesus, I'm working on it." He looked back at his wife. "Which is more than I can say for you, Missy."

"I never said I thought coffee was a sin, so I got nothing to work on," she said.

George had two bright red spots, one on each cheek. His lips were pursed tightly.

It was time for me to start earning my money. "I think I'm getting a sense of how these things get started. But why don't you tell me what your goal is here? What would you like to see happening through your counseling?"

George turned toward me, hazel eyes blazing. "Sweet Jesus, ain't that obvious?" He swiveled toward his wife. "Now don't you say nothing. I know what I said, and the Good Lord knows you push me to it sometimes." Pivoting his whole body back toward me, his chin jutting, George said, "I got to apologize. I don't mean to be getting all bent out of shape here. But, to me, there's only been one goal, all along. I want my wife to come home."

"Okay. How would you like to accomplish that?" I asked.

Both of them stared at me blankly.

"There was a problem that brought you here in the first place. That's why we're here."

"We're here because some dumb a..." George looked at his wife and abruptly changed his wording. "Some knuckle-headed judge said Amanda had to go to Beginnings. It wasn't my choice to be here."

I took a deep breath. Heaven forbid this should be easy. "All right, but do you agree that the way you two have handled conflict in the past has to change?"

"I got no problem here. There's nothing wrong with my self-control," said George.

"Okay, Amanda," I said. "What do you think the goal of this counseling should be?"

She hesitated for once, head cocked. Her tongue thoughtfully outlined the corner of her mouth as she looked at George. She spoke low so that I almost didn't hear her over the music which had changed to Teen Angel. "I know my anger is a problem. I got to stop and think before I do stuff, Dina says."

"So you want to use this couples' counseling to work on ways to handle your anger?" I prodded.

"Well, yes, but..." She threw another look at George as the waitress came up with our order.

"Anything else, Hon?" The waitress asked.

George looked around the table.

I shook my head as I sipped my strawberry milkshake. Amanda raised the coffee cup to her lips with narrowed eyes as though to dare him to say something.

He shook his head. "Looks like you got everything," he said.

"All right," said the waitress. "You just holler if you need anything."

Determined not to let the interruptions of the restaurant derail the counseling session, I spoke up as soon as she left, even though it was hard to talk when my teeth felt frozen from my shake. "You started to say something, Amanda?"

"Yeah," she said slowly, eyes on George. "I'm not the only one who needs this counseling. I don't know yet, if I want to go back home. I've had it with this Jesus stuff. I didn't get married to be told I was sinning just 'cause I drink coffee or want to go dancing once in a while."

George drew his stomach in and his head back. He started to talk through gritted teeth that showed a bit of lettuce from the hamburger he had in his hand. "What we're here for is to help you learn to handle your anger. I want you home, Amanda Jean. No more of this crap. I'll do whatever it takes to help you with that, but I don't see no need to be dragging in the kitchen sink here. I'm not gonna do it."

"You don't like my church, fine. You don't have to go to church. But don't you be dragging it into every blessed argument here because that's not the problem. The problem is when are you going to start acting like my wife and come home?"

I put a hand up to stop the discussion. "At this point, Amanda can't come home until she has worked on her problem. Let's not lose sight of that."

"I been!" she said. "I attended every Gol darn meeting, every counseling session..."

"There has been some feeling among the counselors though, Amanda, that you aren't really engaged in the counseling."

"'Course not." said George, through a mouthful of fries. He swallowed hard, then said, "Didn't she just tell you she don't want to come home? She don't want to try. This way she can say," he raised his voice to a falsetto, "'those counselors don't want to let me come home. I'm going to every meetin'.'"

Amanda sat up abruptly, clattering her coffee cup, spilling some in the saucer. "I've had just about enough, George Vernon Gannon. I don't have to take any more of this. Sure I get mad. I never said I didn't. But at least I don't run around trying to tell the world how they should act. You got a problem too, George, and I've just about had my fill of it." With that, Amanda twisted in her seat to grab her coat then stomped off.

I wiped my mouth with my napkin and watched out the huge plate glass window as Amanda spun off in her little red Neon.

George shook his head and clicked his tongue. "Ain't that always the way?" His voice was matter of fact, but his eyes looked moist.

"George, I'm sorry. Maybe when she thinks about it, she'll change her mind. But I have to tell you, you and Amanda need long term counseling, which Beginnings is not set up to give to you. You need to give some thought to where you will go next if she does want to try."

George stared at his now empty plate. "Where do you go for this kind of thing?"

I stood up, gathering my coat. "I'll be able to give some referrals to Amanda, if she wants them. But there are plenty of places--county mental health among them, that would be able to work with you."

George looked up, eyes bright with unshed tears. "It's not like we got a lot of money. But I'll tell you, I'd give everything I own just to have Amanda back home again."

I nodded and left, tears of sympathy in my own eyes.

* * *

The clouds that had been threatening all day were sending out snow flurries, and my car was cold. I steered toward the mountains that meant the West side of town and home. It had been a long day, but it wasn't over yet. I couldn't wait to get home, but it was Saturday. I had errands to run. The bank and the post office were already closed, but I still had a pile of books to drop off at the library and a mound of dry cleaning to exchange for the one I had to pick up. The kids were already home when I got there.

"You're early," I said as I came into the living room, arms full of library books. RJ lay sprawled on the floor in front of the TV watching "Wide World of Sports". He had all the available pillows in the room scrunched under him, plus the blanket pulled off his bed, so that his skinny blue jeaned form resembled an oversized bird in its nest. I got a glimpse of someone downhill skiing, but it obviously wasn't here in Colorado, because the sky on the set was clear. Hannah was, as usual, in her room with the stereo blasting, probably on the phone.

"How's it going?" I asked.

"All right, Mom. Can you close the door? It's cold."

"How about you go out and get the dry cleaning for me, and then we'll close the door," I said, continuing into the kitchen.

He grunted and clomped out, returning a minute later with the clothes.

"So why are you home early?" I asked, as I sorted my pile from theirs. I looked up to hand him a sweater.

"Dad had a date for dinner," he said, not looking at me.

What a jerk. Couldn't he at least have spent a few hours with his kids? He had the whole rest of the week to spend with his girlfriend. And RJ already felt as though his dad didn't want to be with him. Wait until I got a hold of Roger. I'd give him a date for dinner. He could have at least fed them. They usually ate dinner with him on Saturday. I took a deep steadying breath. "Okay. So you guys haven't eaten?"

RJ rolled his eyes. "Mom, it's only four o'clock."

He knew I hated that. I'd been trying to teach both kids not to do that since they were about three. "Did you get to the library for that report you've got due?"

RJ's eyebrows met in the middle of his forehead as though he honestly couldn't remember. "What report?"

I gave him the benefit of the doubt. "The one on the respiratory system?" I spaced my words out to give him time to remember. "RJ, think. The report you were going to do with that girl you didn't want to tell me about."

Hannah clattered into the room, wearing a big blue sweatshirt and jeans. "He didn't do anything today but hog the TV at Dad's."

"I'll do it tomorrow, Mom," he said.

I'd heard that one before, but the library was closing just as I dropped off our books, so there was nothing I could do.

The phone rang just as I realized that I hadn't planned for them to be home for dinner tonight. I balanced my checkbook in my head, to see if I had enough money left to take them out to eat someplace really nice. It had been a while since we'd done anything like that.

"Mom, it's for you." Hannah's voice interrupted my calculations.

"Hello?"

"Ms. Berreano?" I heard a male voice say. "This is Lieutenant Farrell with the arson investigation squad. I'd like to come by and talk with you."

My afternoon craving for chocolate returned with a vengeance.

Chapter 10

Another coffee shop? The thought entered my mind only to be firmly nixed. But I didn't really want to talk about the fire in front of my kids.

"Sure, you can come now, if you'd like," I listened to myself say.

I heard the rustle of papers over the telephone wire. "Let's see," he said. "I think I know about where you live. I can be there in about ten minutes."

"See you then."

Both kids had wandered into the kitchen after me, scavenging through the refrigerator.

"Hey, guys," I said, looking around to see where I'd laid my purse when I came into the kitchen. "Would you two like to go over to McDonald's and eat? You could bring me something back."

"You mean, like walk?" Hannah said as though that were some painful punishment.

"Yeah, walk," I said. McDonald's was less than three blocks.

"It's cold."

"Hannah, you're too old to whine like that," I objected absently, scrounging in the bottom of my handbag for stray change. Six dollars would not make it.

"But, Mom," she said.

I looked up, putting my this-is-serious expression firmly on my face so I wouldn't get any more protests. "I have someone coming over here to talk to me about work."

Hannah's voice sounded hard. "So you want us to go somewhere."

I shrugged. "Can't be helped."

RJ grabbed for the money in my hand. "What's our limit?"

I reached into my handbag again and brought out my emergency twenty. "Just get filled up," I said, handing it over. "And get me a hamburger and fries."

They were halfway out the door before I thought to yell, "Hey, you're going to need coats."

* * *

I busied myself making a pot of coffee and trying to tidy the place up a bit while I waited.

Farrell looked about the same as he had before. Was that really just Tuesday? His graying red hair looked a little windblown, his freckled nose a bit red from the cold, and he wore dark gray slacks instead of a uniform. But essentially his long lean shape looked just about the same. In his right hand, he carried a small black briefcase.

He stomped his feet as he came into the house, although I didn't see much snow come off his shoes. As I took his black nylon jacket, I saw his eyes make a sweep of my nearly empty living room and wondered briefly what he thought, but then shrugged it off. I had enough to worry about without fretting about whether some middle-aged policeman approved of my post-divorce decor, or lack of it. Still, I was glad that I had bundled RJ's blanket downstairs before Farrell came in.

I steered him into the kitchen. The living room looked as though I belonged to a band of roving gypsies, but the kitchen, with that white pine table, looked like the kitchen of a stable, dependable woman. "Coffee?" I asked.

"It sounds wonderful."

"No partner today?" I asked as I poured us both a cup.

"I didn't think we needed both of us here. Just tidying up some odds and ends," he said, pulling some papers out of his briefcase.

I put the coffee carafe down and sat down myself. "So what can I do for you?"

"I'm trying to make sure I know where everybody was in the house at the time of the fire."

"They were asleep," I said, surprised.

He handed me a floor plan of the house, and I noticed that he didn't wear a wedding ring. Not that that meant anything. I bent over the paper. In each bedroom, he had carefully printed the occupants' names in blue ink. Berreano had been printed over the counselor's office, then in parentheses, Atchison had been added in black ink.

"Does that look about right?"

"Except for Nicky," I said absently. Why was this so important?

"What about Nicky?" He looked up from the papers he was shuffling, his eyes piercing me.

Would you call those eyes blue or gray, I wondered. They were just on the line between. But they were very sharp. He'd suddenly gone from a friendly guy who looked like he had a good sense of humor to a rather scary authority figure. Despite my own suspicions of Nicky, I suddenly felt reluctant to tell this man what I'd learned.

"Nicky and her kids were sleeping in Eileen's room." I pointed out the room on the house plan he'd given me.

"When did this happen? Did you change her room?"

I shook my head. "No. They'd had a fight, so Nicky decided to stay up there."

Farrell pulled his head back as though to withdraw from me, his mouth a straight line, his eyes hard and searching. I felt guilty, even though I knew I was telling the truth. I felt compelled to add, "I didn't know this until after the fire. From what Nicky told me, this happened early on, before I came to work that night."

"I see," he said. He looked back down at his papers, selecting one and scribbling on it furiously. How come when he wrote like that it came out so neatly?

"Did she tell you what happened?"

"Yes."

"And?" He glanced up at me, waiting.

"Didn't she tell you any of this?"

"Not a word. We were under the impression, partly due to you, that Nicky and her children slept in the same room as Mary Ellen. That raised a number of questions as to why Mary Ellen suffered from smoke inhalation, and they didn't. Not to mention why Nicky didn't try to rouse her roommate, and you did."

"Hey, don't blame me," I said, feeling like a fool. "I spent time in that room that night looking for Nicky and the kids." Even as I said it, I wondered how to phrase their fight. It would look really bad for Nicky if I told him that she and Mary Ellen didn't get along at all, and I didn't want to be the one to implicate her.

Farrell put down his pencil and looked straight into my eyes. His were definitely blue--light, piercing, beautiful blue. I always did like blue eyes. Then again, Roger had blue eyes.

"Kaye, you have to realize something here. This is a crime scene. I think you withheld evidence. You never told us about your husband arguing with you in the parking lot of the safe house the night of the fire either, did you?"

"I didn't?" I thought back to that night, but it was a blur. I thought I spilled my guts out, but maybe I didn't mention it.

"No, we got that little bit of information from one of the residents. And of course, you verified it, when Officer Wiloski called to tell you that your Volvo had been found abandoned in a snow-emergency route. But you aren't volunteering anything here. You wait until we pry it out of you. We'll get back to your husband in a few minutes. Right now I want to talk to you about Nicky."

I wasn't being intentionally dishonest. I'd told him everything I remembered at the time. "I think I told you that I didn't remember seeing Nicky in the house that night." It sounded like a feeble excuse even to me, but I felt obliged to defend myself.

Farrell slammed his hand down on my white pine table. "Kaye, a woman has been murdered. Someone, and it is beginning to seem likely now, someone inside the safe house, did it. Now either you know something... or perhaps did something, but I'm going to find that out. Understand?"

* * *

What I understood when he finally finished our interview was that Farrell suspected anybody and everybody, including Mary Ellen, of having set this fire.

The arrival of my kids with my hamburger curtailed the interview. But it didn't stop me from thinking. It seemed like I thought all night.

I knew I hadn't done it. I had my suspicions about Roger and a couple of the women in the safe house, but I preferred to think that none of them had done it. That left Mary Ellen's husband. Even in the middle of the night,

I still couldn't make myself believe that the Crips had set the fire in revenge against someone's girlfriend. After all, it didn't look as though the woman had made it out of L. A.

Tired as I felt, I tossed restlessly on my bed, waiting for morning to come. If Harry had set the fire, Mary Ellen's mother might know something. Suddenly I couldn't wait for my appointment with her Sunday afternoon to return Mary Ellen's clothes.

Sunday morning, Hannah dragged RJ off to some friend's church that had a great youth group. I wondered about this sudden zeal for religion, but put it down to an ulterior motive. After the church service, the youth group was going tubing in Evergreen. The kids would be gone all day.

The skies had cleared, but it still felt brutally cold when I drove to the address given to me at the funeral. I got out of the car and huddled into my red wool coat. I was glad of the warm, wool slacks I wore, as I surveyed the neighborhood.

It looked as working class as the one I lived in, with most of the houses brick bungalows. But all their walks had been shoveled, and there were none of the sleds, bikes, or skateboards that showed children lived in the area. As a matter of fact, the whole neighborhood was deafeningly quiet. It felt a little eerie as I unloaded the boxes from the trunk. I kept looking around, sure that I felt eyes peering at me from behind the curtains of the silent houses.

I took my time, probably because I was too proud and stubborn to want to appear embarrassed by prying eyes. But after making a couple of trips up and down the porch steps, my trunk was empty.

The doorbell seemed to echo out on the concrete porch, and I looked around to make sure I hadn't roused anyone. As I did, I noticed that I had somehow left wet marks from my shoes on the cracked but spotless porch.

I must have picked up snow in the street. I poked at the marks with my toe, trying to erase them before anyone saw.

Mary Ellen's mother answered the door. If I'd thought at the funeral that she looked heavy, I was wrong. Her plain house dress revealed only muscles and good solid bone. She still wore her gray hair molded ruthlessly around her head. Reverend Honecker stood beside her, dressed in what I would swear to be the same cheap black suit he'd worn to the funeral.

I decided to ignore him and turned my attention back to Mary Ellen's mother.

The only sign of her grief was her eyes, painfully reddened against her white face. The tight grip on her mouth forbade me to mention it. I reminded her who I was, giving her Mary Ellen's boxes. She didn't move, keeping me outside on the porch of the little brick bungalow.

I plunged in before she had a chance to slam the door in my face. "Look, Ma'am, I know that this is a terrible time for you, but they're still investigating this fire. Do you think it's possible that Mary Ellen's husband...?"

"He didn't."

She spoke so softly, I had to strain to hear it. She stared at the porch floor. I reached back with my foot guiltily. Surely the wet marks from my shoes were gone by now, but just in case they weren't, I wanted to cover them up. "Didn't what?"

"Harry didn't do it." Her Philadelphia accent, so brisk and nasal, added conviction to what she said. "He was at my house about one-thirty that night, shouting and screaming to beat the band. Thought Mary Ellen was with me. She'd done that before, you know." She looked up at me, eyes haunted. "Wish she'd come here this time."

"Look Mrs. uh..." Although I'd heard her name at the funeral, for the life of me, I couldn't remember it.

"Milford, Ethel Milford. Guess you already know Reverend Honecker, since he was the one took her to that place."

I'd successfully ignored him so far, standing next to her in the doorway. I still didn't like his looks, but I chided myself for having such a shallow attitude. He smiled at me in a politely patronizing way, and I made myself smile back, but I knew the effort didn't reach my eyes.

But Ethel said Harry didn't... "So you're sure it wasn't Mary Ellen's husband?"

Ethel shook her head emphatically. "Harry got hauled off by the cops that night. Cut my phone line one time, so I hurry up and call soon as I see him, now."

But that didn't say anything about where his girlfriend was. Not that I wanted to bring that matter up with his mother-in-law. For that matter, who knew when he got out of jail? Maybe the girlfriend bailed him out quickly. "It must have been an accident then," I said.

Ethel was back to examining the floor, but she heard. "I talked to that Lieutenant Wiloski over to the fire department. He said arson. They thought somebody threw something in through the window 'cause of the burn patterns and all."

I changed the subject. "The thing that's been puzzling me is why didn't Mary Ellen wake up?"

Ethel shrugged.

Reverend Honecker intoned, "It was the Lord's will."

I ignored that, addressing my words to Ethel. "Look, Mrs. Milford, I didn't know your daughter very well."

Ethel burst out, "No you didn't. But let me tell you--she was a good woman, and not just because I raised her that way neither. She was a Sunday school teacher." Ethel looked around wildly as though to see the words she needed, but then picked up steam again. "And she was a member of the church choir--never missed a practice. And she put up with that Harry-- which is more than some would have done, let me tell you." Ethel nodded emphatically. "Then she went to this shelter of yours, and you people killed her."

"We didn't kill her," I protested. Surely this woman couldn't believe that.

"It's the fault of your shelter that Mary Ellen is dead. You people lured her away from her marriage. Me and Reverend Honecker tried to talk Mary Ellen out of going there, but she was stubborn. Said this way, she'd be safe, and Harry couldn't take any of this out on me. And you see what happened."

"It was God's will," Honecker murmured again.

"If you thought that it was against God's will, why did you take her there then?" I asked.

"If the Lord saw fit to give us free will, who am I to argue?"

"But you think the Lord just reached out and zapped her for doing it?"

"Zapped her?" said Honecker, shaking his head. "The Lord is always sorrowful when he must chasten one of his little ones."

He couldn't mean that the way it came out. "You think God set the fire to punish Mary Ellen for leaving her husband?" I asked. I got so hot at the thought that I was glad of the cold on that miserable porch.

"What God has joined..." said Honecker, obviously winding up to give me the full-scale sermon.

I felt no compunction about interrupting. "So you think God did this?"

"God uses many tools and instruments," he said smiling.

"To punish Mary Ellen for some sin?" I couldn't believe this.

"Marriage is sacred." Honecker was still smiling, still serene.

"That is the stupidest thing I've ever heard in my life," I said.

"The Lord often blinds the eyes of all but his chosen," said Honecker.

I left before I could say anymore. In the car, reviewing my lists of suspects, I put Honecker back on the top. He was just loony enough to think he was one of the Lord's instruments.

* * *

The next day I threw on beige wool pants with a cream-colored sweater, hoping the light colors would help my mood. I wasn't looking forward to telling Liz how I'd lost my temper. So, when I came in for work to the little box-piled office at the Red Cross shelter, I wasted no time reporting the whole incident to her. I ended by admitting that I probably hadn't been Beginning's most diplomatic representative.

She shrugged. "It can't be helped now," she said. "Besides, can you imagine if Dina had gone over there and heard him ranting like that?"

Dina worshipped goddesses and loved to wave it in the faces of people who practiced a more orthodox theology. I laughed at the thought, but quickly sobered up. "Honecker is a lunatic. I just can't figure out why if someone threw this--this fire starter, let's call it--in her window, Mary Ellen didn't wake up."

"Sleeping pills."

Now it was my turn to raise my eyebrows.

Liz shook her head and clucked her tongue softly. "Didn't she report it at her intake interview?"

I shook my head. "She told me nothing."

"Well, she took them after the house meeting every evening--never tried to hide them. She told me her doctor prescribed them for her nerves."

That explained the mysterious pills. This must be the medicine that Nicky's kids pulled out of Mary Ellen's purse. I'd never have guessed it. I saw Mary Ellen as calm and cool as possible in a shelter for battered women. Sedatives probably helped.

Chapter 11

Liz had already put her coat on when she remembered to give me the envelope stuffed in the huge black purse she insisted on lugging around with her. "I've been carrying this with me all weekend because I forgot to give it to you on Friday."

My paycheck. Great, I'd been just about to ask her about that anyway. My checking account was definitely low in the water. If we'd been at Beginnings, it would have been left for me in the desk in the counselor's office.

I started to put it in my own handbag without opening it when she said, "You might want to check that. It's been a bit of a shock for some of us. We changed over to that new insurance, remember?"

I tore into the envelope with my fingers. "What the...?" How was I ever going to survive on this? The next paycheck would be even less since I'd gone over to half days after the fire.

Liz nodded. "There has definitely been a mistake somewhere. It looks to me as though they charged us the safe house's portion of the health insurance."

"But I took the kids off my insurance. Roger has great insurance and it's the only thing he's being generous about."

Liz shrugged. "That's just my guess. I've got a call in to the board. They're having their bookkeeper go over it, but we all expected more." Camel hair coat firmly buttoned and belted, she drew her bag over her shoulder. "Do you need help? Can I loan you a little until this all gets straightened out?"

I shook my head, miserably. "I can't. I don't know when I can pay you back. Who knows how long this will go on?" I waved my hand around the room, indicating the Red Cross shelter we were in. At half pay, I wouldn't have any money to spare to repay any loans.

Liz barked a short caustic laugh. "It can't go on much longer. The Red Cross has been wonderful, but we can't stay here forever. These women have to be settled. I've been pushing the fire department for some sort of verdict. We need to get back to Beginnings. And if Mary Ellen was the target, there's no reason why we shouldn't."

"We don't know that."

Liz shook her head wearily. "I know it's hard for you, Kaye. But yes, I'm afraid we do. Her marriage was failing, which would have been against her religion--and his. That makes him a suspect in my book. And if not him...well, no one in this safe house--the only place she had left to go--got along with her. Who knows what other enemies she made? She was the only viable target."

Liz left. Time to check the residents. As I stepped down the hall, the din grew increasingly noticeable. The dormitory room felt stiflingly warm, and the smell of burnt chili hung on the air. Kids were jumping on beds, mothers were scolding them, and the line for the pay phone in the little kitchen was three deep. Nobody wanted to talk to me right now.

Back in the peaceful but overcrowded office, I tried to call Mo at home as I looked over the shift notes. She and Bill had a little money saved for buying a house, and I probably could repay her when the divorce settlement was made. When there was no answer at her house, I tried her work. Sometimes she went in early. I got the trauma department, only to have the phone passed from hand to hand. That was when I started to wonder, what was going on here?

Finally, Sheena, a colleague of Mo's I'd met at Mo's baby shower, told me. Mo couldn't come to the phone. She was upstairs in a room.

"Has the baby come then?" I asked.

"Should be any day now," Sheena said.

"I don't understand. You mean she's upstairs helping a patient get settled?"

"No, no," Sheena said. "Mo was admitted earlier today."

I felt my heart start to pound. Mo wanted this baby so much.

"Is there a problem with the baby?"

"The baby seems fine. This is just a precaution. You really need to talk to Maureen about it."

A precaution? What did that mean? Was Mo okay? "Can you transfer me up to her room?"

"I'm sorry. You'll have to speak to her tomorrow. It's after hours here."

I looked at my watch. Two minutes after eight. Visiting hours ended at eight. That was really picky.

"Look," her voice softened. "All I can tell you is this; Mo's here, she's safe, the baby's safe. We'll take good care of them. Tomorrow's another day. You can call her then." Abruptly her voice became more barbed. "In the meantime, if you want, call Bill. Maybe he can tell you more than I can."

So Bill wasn't there? How strange. No wonder Sheena acted so protective of Mo. Of course she couldn't say much, it probably violated patient confidentiality. I should have thought of calling him myself.

"Thank you." It was hard to say that much with the sudden tightness of my throat. I put the phone down and put my head in my hands.

What was wrong with Mo? I could handle working half time; I'd find the money somehow to support the kids. The suspicions and worry about Mary Ellen's death were horrible, but I knew that it would be resolved somehow. But Mo had always been more than my niece. She was my friend, my support in this divorce, and out of all the people I knew, one of the few people I felt I could really talk to right now.

The door creaked, and I looked up. Amanda stuck her blonde head in the room. "Kaye?" She took in my face and quickly stepped in, shutting the door behind her. "Are you all right?"

"I'm fine." I forced my muscles into a smile. After all, who was the counselor here? "Just a little tired. What are you doing here? I thought you'd be at work."

Amanda pulled up one of the folding chairs and sat down, her feet over the rung, still looking at me intently. "I called in sick. I feel just awful about Saturday."

"Did you mean it? Are you fed up with George?" I asked.

She shook her head, tears glittering in her eyes. "No. He's a good man. I know he is. I just want things to be the way they were. I don't know what to do."

"I just want things to be the way they were." Mary Ellen had said that, the day she came to Beginnings. It was the theme song of the battered woman. But Amanda was the batterer here.

"It looks to me as though you need to make some changes," I said.

"I know. I know," she said. "I will, really, but George can't be all the time pushing the Bible at me. I do want to change though. Will you still counsel us?" She peered at me through wet, dark lashes.

"Is that what you want?"

She looked wildly around the little box-strewn office as though it were a prison. "Yes. I guess. I just want to get out of here. I don't want to end up like Mary Ellen."

I shook my head. I felt so dense tonight. I couldn't understand anything unless it was spelled out. "Why would you end up like Mary Ellen?"

Amanda looked down and fussed with the buttons on her blue wool pantsuit, finally whispering. "Just crazy is all. I think being here made her crazy."

Was that really how Amanda felt about us here? Nobody liked being in the shelter, and I couldn't blame them. It was noisy, crowded, and all too lacking in privacy even under the best conditions. But did Amanda really think we drove Mary Ellen crazy? The tightness in my throat became impossible to speak around.

Amanda put her hand on mine and rushed to reassure me. "Kaye, I'm sorry. I don't mean anything. I tell you, I should just hush my mouth. I don't know what I'm talking about anyway. Just please don't give up on me."

"I won't. If it will help, I can get together with George and you tomorrow afternoon."

Her face brightened, and she jumped out of the chair. "I'll call him right now and let him know. What do you think--will two be okay again?"

"Yes, but please, Amanda, not Gunther Toody's again."

She wrinkled her nose at me. "Don't you worry now. I'll make sure it's some place nice and quiet. Will Crown Hill Cemetery do you?"

I shook my head and smiled. "So we'll be as quiet as the grave? Thanks, that's probably a little too peaceful. Denny's will do."

She laughed and whirled out of the room. The door closed loudly behind her.

I followed her out, ready to do my stuff as counselor.

Most of the residents settled down by ten, and I retreated back to the office for my last hour on shift.

What a mistake. My thoughts chased each other relentlessly around my brain. What happened to Mo? Had I missed the signs that Mary Ellen had been suicidal? What could I do about money? I should never have put that kitchen table on my charge cards. On impulse, I dialed Roger's number to ask for a loan. No answer.

God, if I could just get some of this figured out. Not that I cared where Roger was. And Bill still hadn't called me back, although I'd left my work number on his machine. So I'd have to wait until tomorrow to hear about Mo.

Everything was up in the air. I needed some answers. I started to pace the tiny space between the two desks, the only real floor space in the office. If this thing with Mary Ellen were solved, I would feel better.

It was all starting to make sense, I felt sure, if I could just put it together. Mary Ellen took sleeping pills so she didn't wake up. She never woke up-- not even when this person, whoever he was, opened the window. The window was definitely open.

Lord, that was something I hadn't cleared up with Farrell. He thought I opened the miserable thing. So how did he explain the fact that the window wasn't broken by the thing that started the fire?

"All I need to know then is how the fire starter got the window open," I mumbled to myself. At least I thought it was to myself.

"Mary Ellen did it." Nicky leaned in the door and answered. Her bulky stomach stuck out conspicuously beneath her thin striped shirt.

It was the second time tonight someone caught me off-guard. I was going to have to put bells on that door.

"What?"

"You mean the window to our room, don't you?" she asked as matter-of-factly as though she caught me talking to myself every day. "It sounded like you were talking about the fire."

I nodded numbly.

"Mary Ellen opened the window, took the storm window out and everything," Nicky said. "She said she needed the fresh air to sleep--even when it was so freaking cold." Nicky gave a short bitter laugh. "Another thing to fight with her about. It wasn't right that my kids should freeze just 'cause she had some kind of freaking death wish."

"But what about the alarm system? Why didn't it go off when she opened the window?"

Nicky's brows knit together. "She disabled the thingy."

"What thingy?"

"There's a button." Nicky ran her hand through her short, dark hair. "It's not that hard," she rushed the words. "But Kaye, that's not what I came to tell you. You have a phone call on the other line."

I did? Omigod. What if it were Bill? I needed to hear about Mo. What if he'd already hung up? I ran down the hall toward the phone in the kitchen.

"Kaye?" The voice on the phone was male, breathy and oddly familiar, but definitely not Bill.

"Yes, this is Kaye."

"I warned you. Get those women out of there. I'm not gonna warn you again."

"What?" No wonder he sounded familiar. I remembered all too well the phone call I'd gotten the night Mary Ellen came in. Had I told Farrell and Wiloski about that phone call? This had to be the one who started this fire. We had to trace this call.

"Are you the one...?"

Bang. He hung up in my ear. My heart pounded. Not again. This couldn't happen again. I wouldn't let it. Quickly I dialed star sixty-nine. We had to trace this call. There would be no more Mary Ellens.

Chapter 12

I called Liz first to let her know of the threat to the shelter. She notified our security company and the board of the safe house. I notified the Red Cross's shelter manager myself. She sounded concerned, and said she definitely needed to confer with her colleagues about changing shelters. That was the easy part.

The phone call to the authorities was hard--no two ways about it. I knew I should contact one of the officers already on the case. That meant Farrell or Wiloski. I made sure I got hold of Wiloski. I couldn't cope with Farrell. Even over the phone, I would be able to feel those piercing blue eyes of his.

Wiloski said he'd check into the threatening phone call, but the problem came when I tried to tell him Mary Ellen had opened the bedroom window the night of the fire.

"Actually, after the initial investigation, we determined that you couldn't have opened the window unless, of course, you were the arsonist. The only question was why you told us you did." he asked, his voice openly expressing his skepticism.

"I didn't. You assumed it, when I told you I needed to get Mary Ellen away from the smoke. I couldn't remember exactly, I felt so tired, but it seemed plausible I might have opened the window."

A heavy sigh came over the phone line. "Just where is this leading us?" he asked.

I knew I'd better slow myself down. Even I wasn't sure I made any sense. "I just talked to Nicky, and she said Mary Ellen opened the window."

"If I were Nicky, I'd certainly like everyone to think Mary Ellen opened the window."

"Are you saying you think Nicky did it?"

"We have found her fingerprints on the window."

"She said they argued about having the window open."

"Were these arguments physical in nature?" he asked.

"No! I don't know. I don't think so. Nicky's pregnant."

He grunted. "She's a tough little thing; I don't think anything short of labor itself would stop that one."

That pretty much summed up how I felt about her too, though I didn't want to say that. "Look, you told me to keep you informed," I said. "Now I'm trying to, and you don't believe a word I have to say."

"Did I say that?"

"It certainly came out that way," I said.

"I'm sorry you feel that way," he said.

I lowered my heavily perspiring body onto a metal folding chair. "Are we going to get protection from this guy or not?"

"What guy?"

"The ar-son-ist." I measured each syllable out slowly, then clenched my teeth in order to keep myself from saying more.

"Look, Kaye, there is no evidence that some outsider, some guy if you will, did this. We have no one else's fingerprints on the window, only residents of your shelter."

"How do you explain the fact that the fire alarm didn't go off in that room that night?"

"The only fingerprints on that alarm belonged either to your security company's employees or your residents. It might have been a simple malfunction, which was unfortunate under the circumstances. The other scenario I can envision is Mary Ellen turned it off herself. Now I hear you when you say you got a prank phone call..."

"That was not just a prank phone call. That guy threatened me."

"Sure, sure, I hear you. The thing is, how do we know we don't have some crazy who heard about the fire on the news and decided to get some attention for himself?"

"This guy called before the fire," I said.

"What?"

"I reported it to the police myself. The night of the fire, we got a threatening phone call."

"You never said anything about this before. Tell me about this call."

"I got a phone call that evening, from someone who told me I'd better get all of these ladies home to their husbands."

"Male or female, could you tell?"

"Male," I said firmly. "He whispered, but I could tell."

"Are you sure it's the same guy?"

How did I know? I reviewed the call in my mind. He had said he warned me before, but that didn't mean anything. But his voice seemed familiar. Would I really remember it from one short phone call a week ago? Yes, of course I would, if only because the call had unnerved me so much. One thing I'd forgotten though, and the thought made my heart pump wildly, "He knew my name."

"He called you by name?" Wiloski's voice sharpened.

"Yes, he asked for me. Nicky answered the phone."

"Did he do that the first phone call?"

Did he? "I don't remember. I don't think so."

"But you think it's the same guy?"

"Yes."

"That is interesting. It might take a little time to get the trace information from the phone company. I'll get back to you."

With that, Wiloski hung up.

I kept that phone busy the rest of the night. When the conferencing was over, Liz, the board of trustees of the safe house and the Red Cross came back with a unanimous verdict. Threatening phone calls were a fact of life for a battered women's shelter, especially with the publicity from the fire. We would not move the women that night. The security firm would supply on-site protection, at least until things settled down.

By eleven thirty, with the guard set in place, I was on my way home. I settled into my freezing cold car and tried without any success to warm my cold feet. All I wanted was a quiet house and some time to think.

The house was quiet and filthy. The kids had already gone to bed. It was a school night after all.

But I got a little more to think about. On the jelly smeared kitchen table lay a note from the kids saying that my mother had called. She wanted to know what was going on with Mo and Bill. I wished I knew, and I suspected my mother did. This phone call was her way of keeping me posted. Mary Berreano kept her eye on children and grandchildren alike, even from fifteen hundred miles away. Was there more than Mo's pregnancy that was the problem here? It was too late to call my mother. It was almost two in the morning in New Jersey.

That blasted cot I had in the bedroom had no appeal for me, so I paced the house, picking up after the kids. Hannah's coat, heavy sweater and

French text went in one pile, while RJ's Game Boy, sneakers and socks went in another. I felt tempted to hide the stuff somewhere for a week or so as a consequence for leaving it lying around, but I didn't have the heart to mess with Hannah's French grade. I put the piles neatly at the bottom of the stairs.

I found myself surveying the kitchen with a frown. A frying pan rested in the middle of the greasy stove. On the counter nearby lay a plate with dried egg on it and a bowl full of white stuff. RJ probably had the eggs and jelly toast, I decided. Hannah, back on one of her endless diets, had the salad. I would not clean this up. They needed to be more responsible. I resolved to write them a note complaining about the mess and asking them to clean the kitchen before they left for school in the morning.

But first, I called Dina, feeling ashamed and selfish even as I dialed. She didn't have to be into work until ten the next day, but she would probably be up with the baby sometime tonight. With Mo out of reach in the hospital, she was the only one I knew I could talk to about all this. I poured it all out in a jumble of threatening phone calls: Mo, Wiloski and Mary Ellen.

"So you didn't open the window?" She asked me. This much at least she grasped.

"No. I told you. Mary Ellen did. Nicky said so."

"Man, she must have had a death wish. It was cold."

"That's what Nicky said." I laughed, but my next thoughts sobered me quickly. "I feel so guilty about this whole thing, Dina. If I had just seen that Mary Ellen and Nicky weren't getting along, I would have moved one of them out of that room."

"How could you see if neither one of them told you?"

"I should have known. There was such an age gap, and Mary Ellen didn't have any kids. She wouldn't understand about them."

"You know, there were a couple more counselors in that house besides you. You only work nights. The rest of us could have seen something and changed them around."

"Yes, but these two were my clients."

"Counselors are the worst rescuers on earth," said Dina.

"Meaning?"

"Meaning you're not God, Kaye, or a goddess. You can't know what people don't tell you. You couldn't make it right."

"I know. But I keep thinking if I had, this all might have been different. There might not have been a fire."

"You're acting as though one of them must have set it."

Her words hit me hard, probably because they were true. All the time I protested the idea that Nicky set the fire, did I really believe it myself? No wonder Farrell and Wiloski wondered about this stuff, when I acted as though I thought so, too.

"If neither one of those ladies had anything to do with the fire," Dina said firmly. "All you did by putting them together was give 'em a bad day or two. And even that isn't so horrible when you think that the alternative was to spend it with their abusive husbands."

"Nicky's not married to this guy," I said.

Dina snorted. "Her old man then, Kaye. You know what I mean."

"Yes, I do," I said slowly. "The fire couldn't be my fault if neither one of those women did it."

"Even if they did," she said. "It wouldn't be your fault. You didn't make them do it."

"I know. Thanks, Dina."

"Anytime," she said. "Get some sleep now."

"You too. Good night."

I felt like crying and laughing and singing. For the first time in a week, I didn't feel guilty. I really believed Nicky and Mary Ellen had nothing to do with the fire. Therefore, it wasn't my fault either. Nothing I had done could have contributed to that fire. Why had I needed Dina to point that out to me? Here I had my Master's in psychology, and I needed someone else to point out my irrational thoughts to me.

I slept heavily, but woke early enough to see the kids out the door for school. They'd done the dishes even though I'd forgotten to leave them the note. So then I felt guilty about them, too. I didn't give them enough time or attention.

I didn't feel a bit guilty about side-stepping their questions about their grandmother's phone call though. I told them briefly that Mo had been admitted to the hospital, but she and the baby were both okay. Beyond that, I didn't know what was going on. I didn't know what my mother called about, but if my mother knew more about Mo, or why Bill didn't return phone calls, she should explain it to all of us.

When Hannah and RJ left for the bus, I made a pot of coffee and checked in with the shelter. Liz answered, although normally Brett worked alone until seven. Liz must have been more concerned over that threatening call than she had let on to me last night. Still, her voice didn't betray a thing.

"I just wanted to call to see if anyone found out anything about that phone call last night." I was irritated with myself for my prissy explanation. I don't know why it felt so awkward to me to explain what I was calling about. Of course I wanted to know.

"I'm glad you called," she said. "We're having a staff meeting tonight at five to discuss that, as well as the fire and the safe house's best response."

I felt my stomach knot. The board must have decided to close the shelter down completely, in light of the telephone threats.

Liz continued, "I can tell you this. Lieutenant Farrell pulled some strings at the phone company, and they traced the call to a phone booth, ten blocks away."

"So they really don't know any more than they did before."

"No," she said hardly above a whisper. Then with a false sounding cheeriness, she said, "But we're taking all the necessary precautions. There is really nothing to worry about."

Right. Except for the fact that the arsonist had called last night to warn us again. "I also need to talk to you about my shift," I said hesitantly, wondering if I should even bother; if they were going to close the house. "I think I need to be home more for the kids. Is there a way I could switch with someone, when this is all over?"

"You mean you want to permanently go on day shift?"

"Yes, night shift worked out okay when Roger and I were still together. I had the kids during the day, and he watched them at night. Or he was supposed to." I couldn't keep my voice from sounding a little caustic there, but I didn't care. Liz knew Roger cheated on me while I was off at work.

"Ummm," she said sympathetically.

"Anyway, it worked okay, for a while. But now we're on our own, I think I need more time for the kids."

"Kaye, I can't force anyone to take your shift. But I'll ask around, and maybe we can discuss that at this meeting tonight."

"Thanks," I mumbled. It was the best I could hope for, but I still felt a nervous quiver in my stomach. If no one would change with me, I'd have to quit, and find another job. We couldn't live on nothing. That reminded me, I still had one more thing I needed to ask before I let Liz off the phone.

"I hate to ask, Liz, but have you heard anything about the mix-up on the checks yet?"

"Not a word. I'll get back to you as soon as I know."

Great. In other words, don't count on it for grocery money this week.

Frustrated, I dialed the number of the hospital. They put me through to Mo's floor. "McElreday," said a take-charge female voice I assumed belonged to a nurse.

"Could I please speak to Maureen Preston?"

"I'm sorry," said McElreday. "She's resting right now. Can I take a message?"

"I'm her aunt. I really need to talk to her."

"I'm sorry. She's resting." McElreday's voice sounded firm but patient.

"I see." Disappointment stabbed me. What was wrong? "But is she all right?"

"She's resting."

I wondered hysterically if McElreday was just a recording. I began to suspect she didn't know any other words. "Could you please tell her that her grandmother called and we are all concerned about her?"

McElreday promised, wrecking my theory about recordings. As soon as I got off the phone, I wished my words back. It was bound to be upsetting to know her grandmother called. Mo was very protective of my mother. God knows why. My mother was not only capable of withstanding nuclear bombs, she could light a few herself.

As though to prove it, I called my mother. But it was already almost nine in New Jersey. She was out, probably on one of her endless rounds of volunteer jobs. No luck on reaching Roger either. I got the mop out and attacked the kitchen floor and stewed.

What if they did close the shelter completely tonight? What would I do to support these kids? Worse yet, what if they didn't close the shelter? I had a duty to my children to stay alive.

This guy on the phone sounded like he meant business. They'd better close the shelter. Oh God, it was enough to make me wish Mary Ellen had been suicidal, if the whole thought of suicide by fire weren't so ridiculous.

It must have been nine before I finally did reach Roger--at his office, of course. Normally, when something like this meeting cropped up, I would have had the kids stay with Mo. Under the circumstances, that wasn't possible.

After all, I wasn't asking for much. He'd missed his time with RJ last week anyway. Roger, however, made me feel as though I'd asked for the impossible as I explained my dilemma to him.

"So I won't be able to be home at all from the time the kids come home from school until bedtime. Do you think you could feed both of them and spend some time with them?"

"Kaye, I can't tonight. I'm swamped."

I felt a stab of disappointment. They were old enough to stay by themselves. I just felt they needed some parental time. But if he were busy too, it couldn't be helped. I tapped my fingers nervously on the phone. "Of course; it's tax season. I'm sorry."

"Nooo, it's just..."

"Oh, I see. Belinda." My voice was carefully flat. I didn't want him to know how angry that made me.

"Brenna. Her name is Brenna."

"Does it have to be tonight? Why can't you go out with Brenna another night?"

"Why can't you do this meeting another night?" His voice told me he didn't care if I knew he was mad.

"There's a difference here, Roger. I have to go in for work. You don't. You always said the kids came first."

"Well, of course they come first."

"So you'll spend the time with them tonight?"

"Fine." He bit the word off. "For the kids. But don't think I won't be mentioning this in court, Kaye. This is exactly what I've been saying. You have no time to raise a family with this job you have. And I see no reason why I should babysit for you."

"How can this be babysitting? They're your kids too."

He hung up with a bang. I didn't even get to ask him why the Volvo got towed. Next time.

I bit my lip. But I knew he meant it about the kids' custody. And I wasn't at all sure what I could say in my own defense. Maybe I should let him have the kids. Maybe they would have a better life with him. I sighed and put the mop away. It was time to get cleaned up. I needed to get to Denny's for this counseling session with Amanda and George.

The cold front that had lasted for weeks was finally waning, and the temperature was in the sixties as I walked into Denny's. It was quieter than the last restaurant the Gannons and I had met in, but the waitresses were a lot less colorful. Smoke hung over the restaurant. The smoking section was separate, but just having the puffers on one side of the room and the abstainers on the other didn't help the air quality. My head started to ache even before I got seated, and I knew I'd have to shampoo and wash everything I had on before I went to work that night. To think, when I was a smoker I didn't think people could tell I smoked.

George sat to the side of the restaurant, just over the booth from the smokers. He stood up and waved at me over the heads of the other diners, giving me a glimpse of jeans and a grunge green French tee shirt.

Amanda was nowhere in sight. "Kaye," he said, shaking my hand enthusiastically. "Good to see you. You just set yourself down here. I just know we're going to make some progress here today."

I raised an eyebrow as I took off my coat and slid in the forest green booth, "Is Amanda running late?"

"Oh no." George colored up. "Just in the ladies room."

Poor George. If he were so sensitive that just telling me his wife was in the ladies room made him blush, life with Amanda must be difficult.

Amanda came to the table wearing tight jeans that showed off her athletic figure, and a sweatshirt with Jesus emblazoned on the front. When I saw that, my eyes widened. She obviously dressed to please her husband today.

She smiled a little uneasily, I thought, and slid into the booth next to George just as the waitress came to the table. I let Amanda go first, curious to see if she'd get coffee again. But with a side-long glance under her lashes at her husband, she asked for a Seven-Up. Apparently, she didn't want to upset the mood.

"So, guys," I said, folding my hands on the table as the waitress charged off to the smokier side. "What should we talk about today?"

"When Amanda comes home," said George firmly.

Uh-uh. Wasn't this where the sticky stuff hit the fan in our last counseling session? Maybe he wasn't such a weenie after all. He didn't blush a bit there.

I turned to look at Amanda.

She hung her head and scooted down in the booth as though she didn't want me to see her response.

How strange that she should be the one acting like a wimp. Now what? I cocked my head, trying to peer under the honey-blond hair that covered her face.

"Amanda? How do you feel about that?"

"You know I want to get out of that rat hole, Kaye." She looked up. The face peering out from under all that hair was red. "Sorry, I shouldn't be callin' it that." She brushed her hair impatiently from her eyes. "But I been telling you and telling you. I dearly want to go home. It's just--we got to get some more counseling, don't we?"

"Don't apologize," I said. "I understand what you mean about the safe house. It's hard for anybody to come to a shelter, and this fire has made it even worse for you."

"You got that right," Amanda muttered.

I nodded. "I know. I didn't know getting home was such a priority with you though."

Amanda rolled her eyes. "Didn't I tell you the other day when we were having that fire drill? I been telling you and telling you. You got people in and out all night, driving you nuts. And then last night you go and get another one of those calls. We're all going to be burned alive in our beds. And it won't be the ghost of Mary Ellen that does it neither. I'd have to be crazy not to want to get out of there. The only thing holding me back is this counseling business."

I'd said it before: there was nothing the residents didn't know in the safe house. Of course they'd all found out about the call last night. But I never thought Amanda would take it so hard. And what did she mean about people in and out all night?

"Who's driving you nuts coming in and out all night? You work nights. Is someone complaining about you?"

"Not me, it's that Starr. I stay where I belong unless I got some work to do. She's in and out so much she needs one of them little doors cut in the door, like they got for dogs."

"We have a house curfew," I said slowly.

"You need to be tellin' her that."

"I'm sure she was told when she first came to Beginnings. If she's been taking advantage in the Red Cross shelter after I've left for the night..."

"She took advantage long before that. She was out the night of the fire." Amanda said, as the waitress brought our order. Amanda grabbed her Seven-up and took a swig.

Really? "Where was she the night of the fire?" I asked.

"Out with that boyfriend of hers." Amanda said. "I can't believe you all didn't know. She got back just after I did."

Starr hadn't been with the group in the kitchen that night when I came in, and now that I thought about it, they'd been pretty bubbly. They must have known she was gone, maybe covered for her at the house meeting with Liz. How she'd gotten back was another problem. Someone must have let her in. I remembered the noises I heard in the hall that night that I'd thought was Amanda.

"Are you sure about this?" But I felt certain she was.

"Sure as I'm breathing," said Amanda.

I couldn't picture Starr setting fire to Beginnings, but she'd already admitted to the boyfriend. And who had any information about him? "Do the police know this?"

"Now how should Amanda know that?" George said. "This ain't hardly her problem. You need to ask the police this stuff, Kaye."

It was hard to rein in my thoughts but that wasn't fair to Amanda or George. It was time to get back to the reason we were meeting. "All right," I said slowly. "Let's talk about your options for long-term counseling. You're aware that the safe house is not equipped to give couples' counseling except on this emergency basis." I opened my notebook to give them some referrals.

George cleared his throat. "Actually, I've got that all figured out." He shifted in his seat so he could pull a folded piece of paper from the back pocket of his jeans. "I talked to the pastor of my church."

Many pastors did counseling, but Amanda had been so adamant about not wanting anything to do with George's church that I felt sure I'd missed something here. "About the counseling?"

"Ain't that what I just said?" George asked, smoothing out the paper. "It's all settled. We can meet during my lunch hour, so there won't be no question about cutting into her work time or my work time."

"Are you talking about going to your long-term counseling at your church then?" I asked.

George raised his eyebrows. "Of course. Ain't that what we're talking about here?"

"How do you feel about that, Amanda?" I asked.

"No problem. He wants to do it at his church. We'll do it at his church. I don't care as long as he doesn't try to make me into no Bible thumper."

"Is it a minister you'll be going to, or...?"

George said, "It's a real, certified, honest to goodness, even-been-to-college counselor."

I searched Amanda's face carefully. "So are you happy with that?"

Amanda looked at George with tears in her eyes. "Shoot, it don't make no never mind to me I'll do anything. I got to get home."

I couldn't doubt she was sincere. But I just didn't get it. What happened to the woman who said she'd had her fill of him? Was Amanda really this scared? "Ok-a-y," I said, picking my words carefully. "This is quite a change from our last session."

Amanda said, "I don't know yet if we'll make it, if that's what you mean. I got my reservations. And this counseling," she turned to George, "you know that doesn't come cheap."

The way I translated that was she was scared, but not out of her mind.

"They said they'd work with us on the money part," George said. "Maybe we'll make payments or something. It won't be easy, but we'll make it."

"It will be worth the money," I said.

"Anything would be worth the money to get me out of there." Amanda said.

Chapter 13

After my counseling session with Amanda and George, I ate a quick dinner then rushed over to the shelter. I didn't want to risk being late for this staff meeting.

A counseling intern I hadn't seen since the fire talked to Barbara Washburn, as her kids chased each other around the cots in the main room. She directed me to the little office down the hall.

I was early, and glad of it. The room was hot. I got a seat on one of the boxes by the window. The weekend counselors, plus Brett, and Sonya, the Red Cross shelter manager, flanked me, chatting uneasily as we waited for the meeting to begin. Liz, Farrell and Wiloski got the only chairs. Dina arrived late with a Wendy's Frosty in one hand, and her ski jacket clutched in the other. Her black leggings clung to her heavy thighs, emphasizing every ounce. She was forced to stand, with her back to the door. There simply was no more room.

Dina closed the door, and Farrell stood up. His Dockers and matching black sweater made his eyes look even more blue. The chatter stopped abruptly as we all turned to look at him.

But it was Liz, still seated to his right, who spoke. Looking determinedly cheerful in a bright purple and yellow knit dress, she said, "As most of you know, we had another threatening phone call last night."

Out of the corner of my eye, I saw the weekend counselors, Rene and Nancy, exchange puzzled glances. It didn't look like they had heard anything at all about the call.

Liz continued. "Because of last week's fire, and the death of one of our residents, we felt compelled to treat any threat seriously. We stepped up security on the shelter last night and today. However, we don't believe the phone call to be directly related to last week's tragedy. If anything, the caller was probably attracted by the publicity about the fire."

"How can you say that?" I couldn't stop myself from interrupting. "Are you saying that the fire wasn't arson?"

"Not at all," Farrell answered, not meeting my eyes but looking out over the room. "We know that the fire was arson."

Everybody but me seemed ready to accept that. I wanted to know more. "How?" I asked.

"For one thing because of the V-shaped burn pattern by the window of the downstairs bedroom," he said. "But it has been the conclusion of this investigation that the arson was carried out by Mary Ellen Schuster."

"So you're saying she committed suicide!" I said. "Isn't that a little ridiculous? Who would choose to die by fire?"

Wiloski answered me. "People do all kinds of things that you might consider strange, Kaye. But in this case, we do know that her church appears almost cult-like in its teachings. And we know her minister remains adamant in his belief that shelters for battered women are the work of the devil. Given that we know she came to Beginnings of her own free will, we can only speculate from there."

"So you're saying she purposely did this to destroy the shelter...with her minister's blessing?"

Wiloski shrugged, "We have no evidence that he is involved."

"But you're saying she did this deliberately. Why wouldn't she just leave then? Why would she choose to die?"

Wiloski shrugged again. "She may have been trying to atone for the sin of coming to the safe house in the first place."

"That's just ridiculous. How do you know it wasn't one of the kids playing with a lighter?"

"At that hour?" Farrell answered. "Come on, Kaye. Besides, the accelerant was gasoline. Do the kids around here have access to gasoline?"

"Where would Mary Ellen get it?" I felt the other staff in the room getting restless. Okay, so it wasn't the brightest question.

To his credit, Farrell didn't get sarcastic, but he still looked anywhere but at me.

Liz avoided my eyes too, which told me something else was about to happen that I wouldn't like.

He said, "Anybody can get gas, Kaye. And from what we've been told, Mary Ellen would have had no trouble smuggling it into the house in one of her boxes--and probably did. We found pieces of one of her cartons in the dumpster outside, and we figure the rest of it went up in smoke in the trash can that night."

"As you say, anyone can get gas. I just don't think Mary Ellen did."

He held up one hand, fingers closed. "Kaye, here are the facts. We know it was arson-that's a fact." He held up one finger on the hand. "It is also a fact that the arsonist used gasoline." He put up a second finger, then quickly pointed at me. "Now, do you know something we don't know?"

Now he finally looked at me with his blue eyes full of some emotion I didn't want to identify. I looked away. I kept silent for a minute--unwilling to tell him who I really thought did it. Finally I said, "What about Starr? She and her boyfriend stayed out that night."

Somebody in the room, I thought maybe Brett, gasped. Otherwise it felt clock-ticking silent. Farrell said softly, "I wondered when you would finally break down and tell us that."

I put a hand up. "I didn't know until today."

"You're the night counselor," Wiloski said. "You had to know something."

I shook my head. They really believed that I had been purposely withholding information. Nothing I could say would change their minds. "The important part is you knew Starr was roaming around that night," I said.

Farrell nodded, and a lock of red hair fell over his forehead. "Mrs. Pfeiffer told us herself. We investigated the matter and are satisfied that neither she nor her friend are involved with this arson."

"But Mary Ellen was?" I said.

"That was our conclusion," Wiloski said.

That made me mad, and my voice reverberated stridently. I didn't care. "Don't you see a pattern of phone calls here? I got one before the fire, the fire department got one that delayed their response, and now this one last night."

Farrell's voice overrode mine. "The call to the fire department was subsequently traced back to a couple of teenagers partying that night. They've been charged with criminal mischief."

"What about the phone call I got last week?"

Liz shrugged, "We get phone calls all the time, Kaye."

"You have no evidence that Mary Ellen set this fire," I said. "It could have been the Crips for all you know, out to get revenge on that woman from L. A."

"We've been in touch with L. A. in an effort to check that lead. That woman went back to her boyfriend the night of the fire, and ended up in a hospital for her trouble. There is no suggestion that the Crips had any idea that she would be seeking shelter here in Denver."

All right. I'd never really believed the fire had anything to do with gangs anyway. "Still, you don't know Mary Ellen did it."

"Kaye," Farrell sounded incredibly patient, and could it be, just a little sorry for me? "I know you don't want to believe this, but the facts are pretty clear. We have no one else's prints on the window, but Mary Ellen's and Nicky's. No one else's prints are on the alarm system, but Mary Ellen's and some security guard's. The common denominator there is Mary Ellen. Also the fire was set in the waste basket, just inside the window, where the breeze that night would be sure to fan it. It was not thrown in. It was set. Mary Ellen was the only one in the room. And," here his voice sounded louder, as though trumpeting the final telling detail. "Her husband and her mother agree that she was depressed."

"Her mother never said Mary Ellen would commit suicide," I said, aghast. Ethel would find that as big a sin as leaving Harry. I firmly believed that Ethel would have died herself before she said that.

"She has admitted that Mary Ellen was upset; she wasn't herself," Farrell said.

"Of course Mary Ellen was upset. Anybody would be upset. Her spouse was abusive and their marriage was breaking up. Just coming to a shelter for battered women is upsetting for any woman." My voice rose an octave, but I didn't care. I had to convince him.

"Kaye," he said softly, his face sincere. "Unless you can bring us some new evidence, this investigation is over."

Brett leaned over me to whisper something in Rene's ear. Rene's big wide eyes clung to mine the whole time. What else could I say? Nothing. I had no new evidence. I'd told everything I knew. Suspicions were not evidence. But I knew Mary Ellen could not have committed suicide.

Liz broke into my racing thoughts. "We've been fortunate in that the repairs outside of that one bedroom were pretty minimal. We will keep that room closed, of course, until we've had a chance to fully restore it. But for the rest of the house--the painters were in over the weekend and the carpet cleaners came early today. We're anticipating that we should be able to vacate this shelter by Thursday."

A ragged cheer went up from Sonya and the staff around me. Dina tilted her head toward me and tried to smile.

Liz waited for the noise to die down. "I know that you'll all be glad to get back to Beginnings. We need to plan thoroughly to make this transition an easy one for our residents. And of course, we'll need help with the move. I'm asking all of you to please give us your spare time for the next couple of days to help out."

Rene and Dina groaned. Liz went on as though she hadn't heard, "Luckily our numbers are down, so there is no need for the downstairs bedroom, but..."

I tuned out. I couldn't believe this. Sure it turned out easier for the shelter if Mary Ellen had committed suicide, but saying it didn't make it true. Ignoring the phone calls and the threat to the shelter seemed pretty reckless to me--no, not even reckless--insane. I couldn't go along with this. I didn't want to be there at night, responsible for the safety of these residents.

The meeting ended. People started to stand up and stretch. We were definitely going back.

"Kaye." Liz left her chair to stand in front of me. "Let's go get some coffee."

I wanted badly to decline, furious with her and feeling that she should know that. She'd admitted to pressing for an end to this investigation, and by doing so, she was putting the residents in danger. Besides, I'd had more than enough coffee lately.

Then Farrell appeared and took my arm, looking at me with impassive eyes. "Yes, ladies, let's."

"But I'm on duty," I protested. But I didn't shrug away from him.

"Go on, Kaye." Dina gave me a shove. "I'll cover for you. You could use a break." She inclined her head toward Farrell and gave me an approving thumbs up.

I glared at her over my shoulder as I went out of the room on Farrell's arm. Yes, I agreed, he was cute, but why would she think I wanted to have coffee with him--especially now? She smiled and waved happily at me.

Fine, I'd go to coffee and talk. But neither Liz nor Farrell would like what I'd have to say. I turned my head and straightened my shoulders, setting my mouth in a firm line.

We ended up at the diner down the street in an orange booth whose peeling upholstery had seen better days. Farrell sat down next to me, forcing Liz to take the seat across from us. It struck me that it should be the other way around. Liz and I, the two co-workers, should have been on one side, and Farrell, the outsider, on the other. When I glanced at Liz in question, she looked toward Farrell with raised eyebrows, and smiled at me.

So Liz thought he was cute too. I wondered if Farrell wanted to sit next to me because he was as attracted as I was, or for another reason. Attraction or no, I was going to be honest. Maybe he wouldn't want to be so close after he heard what I had to say.

The waitress took our order, popping gum the whole time, red fingernails at odds with her bright pink tee shirt. She left with a final pop of gum.

I followed her with my eyes. How much did waitresses make these days, anyway? I might be about to find out. Taking a deep breath, I leaned forward to look Liz in the eyes. "You can't do this. You're putting the whole safe house in danger."

"Kaye, I'm sorry," Liz said. Her wide clear eyes and straight-held mouth told me that was true. She'd made up her mind, but regretted that her decision upset me.

Farrell interrupted, "If you know more than you've told us about this fire, you need to make that clear now."

I turned around in my seat, ready to get in his face. "That's been your line all along," I said. "You think if I knew who did this, I wouldn't have told you by now? It's my butt on the line in there at night."

He put his hand on my shoulder to make me look at him, which I almost had to do anyway considering how close he was to me in the booth. With his grip on my arm, it was impossible not to.

His blue eyes returned my gaze steadily. "You have consistently withheld information throughout the investigation. Yet you insist that Nicky or your ex-husband and now Mary Ellen couldn't have set that fire. My take on that is that no one you know could set that fire. But you keep coming up with kernels of information that you've neglected to tell us. You could hardly blame me for suspecting you know more than you've told us."

"I know nothing except reopening Beginnings is a mistake. This guy called me again last night. He threatened me. Whether you want to admit it or not, I believe he will come back, and I don't want to be there."

The waitress chose that moment to come back with our coffee, probably attracted by my raised voice.

My breath came hard as though I'd been running. I made a conscious effort to calm down, leaning back in the booth to let the woman set the cup in front of me.

Even so, she spilled the coffee as she set it down. She set cups in front of Liz and Farrell, and sauntered off without a word.

I concentrated on that plain white stoneware cup with the coffee sloshed in its saucer, trying to compose myself. My anger was doing me no good.

Liz leaned forward and touched my arm just below where Farrell was holding it.

He flushed and let go of me.

I smiled at the thought of his embarrassment and turned my attention to my boss.

She said, "Actually, you've raised a point that I wanted to talk to you about, Kaye. I'd like you to switch to days for a little, help me with this move."

"Okay," I said slowly. Somehow this didn't feel as though it were the answer to my problem about changing shifts. Did she mean permanently or right now?

Liz answered my unspoken question. "I asked the other counselors, and they have all--even the weekend staff--volunteered to take one night each week. That would leave you with one night a week."

"So would I go back to forty hours a week?" I asked slowly.

Liz nodded and smiled brightly; her pink lipstick lent a cheerful emphasis to her face. "Yup, because you'd be working Saturday days. You could have Sunday and Friday off," she added.

Roger had both the kids on Saturdays anyway. It might work. A wave of relief flooded me. But an unwelcome thought intruded. Was Liz trying to make up to me for the shelter's re-opening by rewarding me with longer hours and the schedule I wanted? I tapped a finger uneasily on the table. "It would help me out a lot," I hedged.

"But they can't make the change just yet."

That was fine. I hadn't agreed to it yet either.

"At least not right away," she continued. "Brett's got that night course at UCD. Maybe in a couple of weeks or so."

I nodded, still not committing myself.

Liz hurriedly said, "But I thought about this. It's not really necessary to have a counselor on at nights anymore while we're still at the Red Cross shelter. They'll still have the shelter manager on duty. And I really will need your help with this move. So you could start tomorrow."

God! She was definitely trying to sweeten this deal for me. Her mind was made up. She was willing to make a lot of concessions to get me to change mine.

But she was making no attempt to address the issue of safety in the shelter. I let my eyes telegraph my feelings, conscious that I would do the remaining women in the shelter no good by letting all my feelings out and getting myself fired.

"I think," she said. "It's important for you to get away from this whole situation at night. As a matter of fact..." She paused as though suddenly struck by a bright idea. "Why don't you take a vacation? You have a couple of weeks coming, and by the time you get back, we'll have the shift change you want all arranged. Brett's class will be over and you'll only have to work one night a week." She took a sip of coffee and her lipstick stained the cup's rim.

God, yes. A vacation. I should have thought of it myself. Just what I needed--time to spend with Hannah and RJ; sort out this thing with Mo. No way Roger could say I wasn't spending enough time with the kids this way. I'd be with them until I got my shift change, and then I'd only be gone while they went to school. The perfect solution. Immediately, I felt ashamed of my selfishness. What about the residents who couldn't get away from the shelter until this all was over?

And how could Liz blatantly bribe me like this? After all, just a minute ago, she was saying she needed help with the move. Now she was telling me to take the time off.

And the worst part was that I wanted to. I wanted to just let this whole thing get resolved, and then come back when it was all over. I knew somehow that it would all be over soon. A vacation sounded so good.

But I shook my head, making an effort not to bare my teeth and scream at Liz. "I can't."

Liz arched a sandy brow, and although I concentrated on her, I felt Farrell's gaze on me too.

"I'll come in during the day for the next two days, if that's what you want. I'll help with the move. But I won't change shifts yet, and I won't go on vacation."

I looked Farrell full in his amazing blue eyes to show him I meant business. "I don't want anybody else in there when this guy comes back."

Chapter 14

The next morning started early. I mean really early. The phone rang at three a.m. I stumbled out to the kitchen, barely beating Hannah's anxious hand to the phone.

"Kaye?" asked Mo's voice. I knew that much even after only two and a half hours sleep.

"Mo, what's going on? I've been trying and trying to get hold of you. Are you all right?"

"I just had the baby, silly." Mo sounded amused.

"You did? You mean you just did?"

"At one fifty-eight this morning."

Hannah, dressed only in a sleep shirt with oversize hands emblazoned on the front, stage-whispered to me in our dark kitchen. "What's the matter, Mom? Is Mo okay?"

I reached out and smoothed Hannah's tousled blonde hair. "Mo had the baby."

Hannah's half-shut eyes flew open. "She did? What did she have?"

Mo heard, because she laughed and said, "I had a girl-- seven pounds, six ounces. Her name is Sara."

I mouthed "a girl" to Hannah, before I said into the phone, "And everything's okay? She's healthy?"

"She's just fine. I have her in my arms right now." Mo paused, apparently for my reaction, but I couldn't respond just then. With everything I needed to ask, I couldn't figure out where to start.

She said softly, "Really, Aunt Kaye, you can come see for yourself if you want, later on today."

Mo only called me Aunt when she thought I was being a pain in the butt. I'd better not push it. After all, I could see if she and the baby were okay when I got to the hospital. "You got a deal," I said. "Do you want me to call anyone for you?"

"I think we've got it covered. I called Mom and Dad. Bill called his folks, and Mom said she'd call Grandmom Mary for me. And of course, everybody at work knows."

She laughed again, and I finally felt the tension in my shoulders ease. She'd had the baby, and she and the baby were all right.

"Is your Mom coming out to see the baby?" I supposed I should feel guilty that I didn't know this about my own sister, but I didn't. I didn't need the added expense of long-distance rates right now, and the family jungle drums beat faster than the phone lines anyway.

"Not yet. We asked everyone to wait a week or two, so Bill and I have some time with the baby on our own. Then Bill's mom will come in next month."

Too strange. My sister happened to be wildly enthusiastic about the baby, and she would love to come in and take over the cooking and cleaning while Mo rested. Still Mo wasn't great at resting; maybe it was wise of her.

"Get some sleep and then get that baby ready. I'll come to see you as soon as they'll let me in."

"I can't wait to see RJ's face," Hannah said when I got off the phone. "He bet me it would be a boy."

"Whoa," I caught the tail of her night shirt as she headed towards her brother's bedroom. "You can tell him tomorrow."

Hannah's face fell. "He'll be upset, Mom. He wants to know, too."

"He will know. Later, when he gets up."

"Mother, I can't believe you." Hannah's voice went up an octave and at least three decibels, a sure sign, if I didn't already know it from her calling me "Mother", that I was going to hear it now.

"The next thing you know, you'll be saying we can't go see Mo until after school today."

"I think the baby will keep," I said mildly.

"Mother!" she wailed.

"Hannah, it's too early in the morning. Go back to bed."

She gave me a look that I felt certain was supposed to pierce my hard heart, if not strike me down dead, but she went. I turned the TV on low and settled on the cushions in front of it, carefully tucking my flannel nightgown down around my feet in the night-cold house.

The late-night reruns couldn't hold a candle to the thoughts running through my mind. Here I'd been so worried about Mo. All for nothing. There must have been some little complication and her doctor got worried about a malpractice suit. Everyone is sue-happy anymore. Now that the baby had arrived, I could let go of all the worry. It all turned out okay.

I had to get some sleep. But I couldn't. I needed to pay some bills. I couldn't do that either. Why hadn't bookkeeping fixed that mess with the paychecks yet? I couldn't be the only one complaining. Everyone had bills to pay.

What put me in such a bad place for money anyway? I couldn't really blame it all on Roger. I had let him take the house and all of the furniture. I hadn't said a thing about the money in the bank. I let him do it because I felt he'd earned it. But I was raising his kids. I couldn't do that on nothing. Furthermore, the only reason Roger made the kind of money he did was because I'd supported him through college when we were first married. I'd stayed home when the kids were little, but that was a mutual decision. Why should I feel guilty for it?

If I couldn't do anything about Mo or the safe house, I could at least get my personal life in order. I needed to get this divorce back on track. First thing in the morning I would call my lawyer, Merv Rosen.

I had to work to make this divorce okay. I'd been naive to expect that Roger would play fair with me. Just because he didn't want the divorce didn't mean that he wouldn't look out for himself first and foremost. I wasn't a priority. I hadn't been for years. That left it up to me to make sure I got what I had worked for, not just for my sake, but for the kids'. And I knew just what would make Roger more cooperative.

I leaned back on the cushions and spread my arms wide. If only that mess at the safe house would resolve itself, we could get things back to normal. I didn't want to be there alone with the residents and have the arsonist strike again. I thought of those panic-stricken moments in Mary Ellen's smoky room when I tried to drag her out of bed. Never ever again. I didn't want anyone else to have to go through that either.

No way Mary Ellen committed suicide. Because of the fingerprints, Nicky seemed the likeliest suspect. I still didn't much care for her attitude towards Mary Ellen's death, but I knew Nicky didn't do it. Despite what Amanda told me this afternoon, I doubted strongly Starr did it. Breaking house rules and burning the place down were two different things.

The fact that the Volvo had been left downtown the night of the fire could make me suspicious about Roger, except I didn't think Roger cared enough to torch the safe house. I'd kept in mind what Mo said about the good Reverend Honecker, especially since I didn't like him myself. But I didn't see how he would have known which room was Mary Ellen's room to set a fire. It looked like it had to be someone who knew the place well--someone familiar with Mary Ellen's habits. No, I had to face the one thought I had avoided all day. What if Amanda started the fire?

The evidence seemed so obvious and so damning. She'd been up late for work that night. So if I'd heard her, she could have claimed, as she had on so many nights before, that she felt hungry. Mary Ellen's room was just in back of the kitchen--handy for fire starting. Plus Amanda was the only resident who couldn't leave the safe house by her own free will, thanks to that judge who remanded her here. Yet she wanted badly to go home. But if the safe house were damaged or dangerous? That might be a different story.

Not that I thought she wanted to kill Mary Ellen. Amanda just hadn't thought that far ahead. She probably figured, if she figured at all, that the fire alarm would wake Mary Ellen up. I was willing to bet that like most news in the safe house, it was common knowledge that Mary Ellen liked that window open. Amanda must have reasoned that the open window would make people think it was someone outside the shelter who started the fire. She hadn't counted on Mary Ellen dying. Amanda was trying to point the blame away from herself. That was why she acted so weird lately.

I needed to talk to Starr. And I wanted to talk to Barbara Washburn's kids again. They'd said they heard something that night.

Okay. So I would get the kids off to school, visit Mo, see my lawyer, and then go into the safe house. I wouldn't want anyone to think I wasn't doing my part for this move.

All that resolved in my mind, I fell asleep on the cushions in front of the TV, and only the kids getting ready for school made me get up. Then I wished I had gone back to bed after the phone call. My legs were so full of pins and needles from being folded up for hours, that I had to hobble to get dressed. Plus I had to deal with RJ and Hannah.

"Why can't we stay home and see the baby?" Hannah asked.

"We've already talked about it," I said. "This baby will be around a long time."

"Yeah, right," said RJ.

"What? You're afraid it's going to walk off? I don't think so," I said.

"Mom," said Hannah, rolling her eyes. "You know what we mean. We just want to go see her."

"I'll take you tonight," I promised, kissing her on top of her head. "We'll take the camera and some magazines for Mo and a present for the baby. Okay?"

"Yeah, then you'll say we need to get home, it's a school night," RJ said.

"Nobody stays a long time when they visit someone in a hospital."

That seemed to reassure them. Don't ask me why. They went out the door ten minutes later. I ducked into the bathroom for a quick shower, then I called Merv. It was too early even for his receptionist, but he was there just as I knew he would be. He'd see me for a quiet lunch in his office--secretary catered. With that settled, I was off. I arrived at the hospital when visiting hours began.

The room was dark with all the curtains closed. My eyes couldn't adjust after the morning sunlight and the bright glare of fluorescent lights in the corridors.

"Knock, knock," I said, not sure about which partition was Mo's.

"Kaye? Is that you?" Mo's voice came from around the first curtain.

I stumbled a little in the darkened room and banged right up against the clear plastic port-a-crib. Oh no, the baby.

"I've got her," Mo said, her face angled toward me. She didn't rise from her pillows.

I squinted to see her better in the shadowy room. She'd tried--she had her makeup on even if she had applied it with a heavy hand. Even makeup couldn't hide the fact that she looked pale, with purple circles under her eyes. Her usually beautiful dark hair looked stringy with dried sweat. She looked exhausted. I remembered feeling that tired and achy from having my own two kids. My mother always said you forgot that part the moment you held the baby. I never forgot. But it was normal. I felt my last strand of worry finally let go. Mo looked okay as far as I could see.

"She's sleepy," Mo said. "I know how she feels too. I had such a rush of adrenaline right after I had her. Now I can't keep my eyes open. Want to hold her?"

I did, of course. Sara was a typical newborn, which is to say she looked like W. C. Fields or Winston Churchill. Naturally, I told Mo she was beautiful. Hannah was born with a pointed head and red peeling skin. I thought she was gorgeous.

A nurse came in to take Mo's vital signs, and another came to fuss over the baby. It was too big a crowd for such a small cubicle. So I kissed and hugged, oohed and aahed, and took my leave even quicker than I told the kids I would. I didn't even realize until after I left the hospital that I hadn't seen Bill. He must have gone home to get some sleep.

Even though it was still morning, it felt much later. Clouds hung darkly overhead. Rain fell in small icy-hard drops as I dashed into the big brick church that housed the Red Cross shelter. Even huddled in my coat, I felt chilled. So much for our big warm up. It didn't rain in Colorado in January. I knew, even without listening to a weather report, that the rain would soon change to snow.

Inside it felt much cheerier and brighter. I heard the clatter of dishes from the small kitchen. The smell of toast floated in the air. Nicky and Amanda chatted and laughed together as they folded clothes. Nicky's kids, catching their mother's mood, giggled and chased each other around the room. Obviously, they liked moving back to Beginnings.

I caught Liz by her sweater-sleeve as she went by with a box of blankets. "How can I help?"

"You can do the exit interview for Starr," she said. "Everything else is under control."

"Exit interview?"

Liz nodded, "She decided to move in with a friend of hers."

"She's not going back with her husband?"

"She says not."

Was Starr going to stay with the guy who had no room for her daughter? "So what's the rush?"

Liz shrugged, a gesture made more awkward by the box she carried. "She doesn't want to go back to Beginnings."

Me neither. The arsonist knew the location of Beginnings. Despite my worries about Amanda, I still had some hope that the arsonist was someone from outside the shelter. And that he hadn't figured out how to reach the Red Cross shelter yet. This exit interview was my chance to talk to Starr and see how realistic that hope was. I knew from my last talk with her that Starr was hiding something about the fire. I nodded at Liz and moved toward the kitchen to find out what.

Starr shut the dishwasher door as I walked into the room. Her tight black spandex leggings and low-cut body suit highlighted her figure. It looked like cheap bar wear, but Starr wore stuff like that all the time. I always wondered why women who dressed like that didn't get cold. She wore her blond hair piled on top of her head, with just a few strands strategically placed to escape.

"Hey, how's it going?" I asked.

She smiled, "All right, I guess."

"I hear you're moving out."

"Yeah," Her smile became a little more guarded as though she expected a lecture. I felt my heart sink. She must be moving in with the jerk who wanted her daughter out of the picture.

"So tell me about it."

Starr wiped her hands on a dishtowel hanging from the cabinet door, then turned and leaned against the cabinet, eyeing me carefully. She twisted a loose curl around her index finger. I stared at the decals on her nails. Impossible as it seemed, it looked like she had the whole zodiac on her fingers.

"There's not much to tell really," she said.

"Is this the guy you were talking about before?"

She frowned.

"You told me a couple of days ago that you had a friend who could take you in, but he didn't have room for your daughter."

"Oh yeah."

"So where will Aleia go?"

"I've decided not to put her through all this upheaval. She'll be happier with her father. Then she can stay in the same house, go to the same school, and be with her friends." Starr's face shone with earnestness.

I wasn't buying it. "Do you really think it's a good idea to return her to a man that we know is abusive?"

"He is her father." Starr sounded sulky and defensive.

"And he has a history of violence. How do you know that he won't abuse her?"

"He's never been as bad to her as he was to me."

"Starr, don't give me this garbage. What has gotten into you that you are willing to put your daughter into a possibly dangerous situation so you can play house with this guy? He can't be that cute."

"The stars are telling me to make a change."

"Leaving your husband wasn't a big enough change?"

Starr shook her head. "You don't understand. My readings clearly show that Beginnings is not a safe place for me."

"I see." I moved toward a stool at the counter, and motioned her along side of me. I didn't put much stock in astrology, and I didn't understand how the stars could warn her about a specific place. Yet Starr seemed serious, and I wondered if the threat had come from someplace other than a reading. "Starr, when I asked you the other day if you had seen something the night of the fire, you seemed evasive."

"I did not. I told you, I didn't see anything wrong with Mary Ellen."

"Was there something wrong somewhere else?"

Starr dropped her eyes to her lap and rubbed her hands back and forth over her thighs.

"What was it, Starr? I know you were out that night, but I'm not here to talk to you about breaking house rules. You had more opportunity than anyone of seeing anything wrong, and now you want to leave."

She looked startled. "What about Amanda?"

"What about Amanda? Do you know something I don't?"

Starr eyed me consideringly, her teeth sunk in her lower lip. The effect was about the same as if she'd put her hand over her mouth. I definitely got the feeling that she'd said something she shouldn't. "I saw Amanda that night," she said slowly.

I nodded. "Yes, she came in from work just before you got back, if I have my times right. You must have been the noise I heard in the kitchen, and she must have let you in. Is that right?"

Starr shook her head. "Not her--Eileen. She looked after Aleia that night for me and let me in. We crouched in back of the refrigerator when you came in." She cocked her head as though to evaluate my reaction.

I shook my head. I didn't understand. So what did this have to do with Amanda seeing something wrong? "So you saw Amanda upstairs after you got in and she got done with work?"

Starr frowned and then blurted out. "That's what I'm trying to tell you, Kaye. Amanda didn't go to work."

Chapter 15

I took a moment to take that in. Of course Amanda went to work. She'd come home at three, hadn't she? But that didn't mean she'd gone to work, did it? Now that I thought about it, I had never been at the safe house when Amanda left for work. She always left before I got there. But that night Amanda drove away as Roger and I argued in the parking lot. But what, if anything, did this have to do with the fire?

"How do you know she didn't go to work?" I asked.

Starr looked nervously around, and I remembered I'd seen Amanda in the other room. Was Starr afraid of Amanda? "I saw her."

I rolled my arm in that motion that said get on with it.

"We ran into her at One-Eyed Willy's," Starr said. "Dancing with some cowboy."

Who, I wondered, was the cowboy? "Why, Starr, I didn't know country music was your thing," I drawled.

She smiled. "It's not really, although I like it better than rap. My, er--the man I was with, likes country."

"So the other day when I talked to you and Naomi, you didn't want to tell me about Amanda?" I asked.

Starr shook her head. "It wasn't that, really. I didn't tell you this because I didn't want to get thrown out of the house."

"Because of curfew."

"Yes."

"You told the police?" It wasn't a question really. I figured if she'd told the police she'd gone out that night, why not tell them Amanda had too?

"Nooo."

Should I tell Farrell? Oh screw it, he'd figure I'd known all along, and he'd still think Mary Ellen set the fire. "Why not?"

Starr shrugged. "I don't know."

"Are you leaving because you're afraid?"

She wouldn't meet my eyes, just kept running her hands over her thighs. "I told you, the stars say it's time to make a change."

I could see I wouldn't get any more out of her. I sighed and waved her toward the office. "Come on. Liz asked me to do your exit interview."

When I finished the interview, I realized I had missed something. I put a hand on her black sleeve as she stood up, about to leave. "You said Amanda had more chance to see something than you?"

"No, I didn't."

I'd realized by then that I had to watch how I phrased things with Starr. If I didn't state things precisely right, she took the opportunity to slide out from under. "I said you had the best chance to see if anything was wrong the night of the fire and you said, 'What about Amanda?'"

Starr hunched her shoulders and her brown eyes darted around as though she were an animal seeking shelter from a predator. She didn't find the hiding place she was looking for. After a minute, she sighed and said, "I just meant she was out there too."

"Was there something out there to see?" I asked, abruptly remembering my belief on the night of the fire that someone was watching from the backyard. Another detail I hadn't told Farrell. I wondered if Alzheimer's ran in my family. My mother seemed to have all her marbles in one secure place, but I sure forgot a lot of important things.

Starr shook her head, still not looking at me. "I don't know. I didn't see anybody. But it was snowing pretty hard by then, and I thought..."

She stopped and I squirmed impatiently. Thought was not something I connected with Starr. "You thought what?"

"I thought this car followed me back to the safe house." She took her time, eyes squeezed shut as though remembering. "The bar closed, and everybody left. And this car, it wasn't right in back of me, you know, but the streets were empty since it was so late. It just seemed like it made every turn I did." She shivered a little, and finally turned her face toward me. "I figured it had to be Amanda, you know. Still it made me nervous."

"Did you see what kind of car it was?"

Starr shook her head.

"How about the color; anything to make it stand out in your mind? I know it was dark."

"It was a car," she said. "It was dark. The only thing I saw different about it was that one of its headlights was out."

When I was a kid, we called them pididdles, and we would count them on long trips at night. It was surprising how many of them were around. It wouldn't exactly help identify the car. "Did you see Amanda get out of the car?"

Starr shook her head. "It went up the block to the Seven-Eleven. I figured she'd forgotten something."

I shook my head. Amanda came home before Starr. So maybe this car was just a coincidence--had to be. Any woman could get spooked out alone at that time of night. Unless... "You don't think it was your friend, wanting to make sure you got back all right?"

She shook her head, not looking at me again. "He's very protective of the ladies in his life. I worked up his astrological chart for him, and it was one of the first things to come out. But I told him this place is a secret."

Spoken like someone who might have to return to the safe house or who at the very least didn't want to get in trouble there. So I could take my pick. Her pursuer very well could have been some guy who ran out of toilet paper in the middle of the night or it could have been Starr's latest conquest. But it didn't look like it could be Amanda.

An hour later, I said goodbye to Starr and Aleia as they climbed into their car. It was one of those little boxes customized with a psychedelic paint job and a crystal hanging from the rearview mirror.

It felt even colder than it had that morning. The rain mixed with snow, which blew under my collar and gave me the shivers.

Aleia fluttered a pudgy hand, smiling shyly at me through the car window. She looked happier than I'd ever seen her. The car started with a sputter, and my throat tightened. I wanted to snatch Aleia from the car and take her somewhere she'd be safe and cherished. Starr gave me a tight smile and pulled out of the parking lot.

The day dragged on, and I caught myself checking the clock constantly. As more residents returned to the shelter, the noise and the energy level increased. Dishes clattered in the small kitchen. Children banged in and out of doors, letting in gushes of icy air. The phone rang continually with crisis calls. I got caught up in the commotion. I found myself drumming my fingers or tapping my feet. I needed to calm down, but I couldn't.

One thought gnawed at me. Some innocent Red Cross volunteer shelter manager would be alone in this shelter with these women tonight and all because I had let Liz persuade me she needed me during the day today. Now I felt guilty. I tensed at the thought that the arsonist was still out there. No one would be on guard because everyone else thought poor Mary Ellen was the arsonist. I clung to the idea that everyone would be safe here--surely the address of this Red Cross shelter couldn't be known to whoever started the fire.

It was dark outside the windows when Liz left. I was in the middle of explaining to a woman on the crisis phone that it would be better if she left her abusive husband before she got hurt again. "I know you want your kids to have a dad and a mom, Gina," I said as Liz waved goodbye and walked out of the office. "But what will happen to your kids if he kills you next time?"

"He wouldn't kill me," she said. "He didn't mean to break my wrist. It was an accident."

I hung up a half hour later, totally wrung out. I still wanted to talk to Barbara Washburn before I went home. I was due to be relieved at six. I only had twenty minutes left. I lifted my tired body from behind the desk, hoping Barbara had returned from work.

I found all of the kids lined up in front of the TV, including the Washburn kids. Barbara must be around.

It took a minute, but I finally spied her sitting on a cot in the main room going through a suitcase. It was a bit of a shock to see her in a wool suit and silk blouse; all clearly designer quality. She'd always worn sweats and jeans before. It took me a minute to recognize her. Her hair was brushed back to reveal gold hoop earrings. Her creamy dark skin glowed with blusher to match her power-red lipstick. "Hey, how's it going?" I asked.

She looked up. The shadows under her eyes revealed her fatigue. "Hi, Kaye. It's going okay. What can I do for you?"

"What do you do?" I asked, before I could stop my mouth. I felt like a real fool. Why didn't I just come right out and say hey, Barbara, I've never seen you look this good before? "I know you work in a bank, but doing what?"

"I'm vice president of loan services," she said. She smiled a calming smile, fully aware of my discomfort and trying to soothe me. "I have to look like this for work," she fingered her skirt. "But when I'm off, I like to kick back."

"At least I know now who to go to when I need money," I said.

She smiled again, but I felt her exhaustion. I'd better get on with it.

"Listen, I've been thinking about our conversation in the kitchen after the fire. You said you heard Mary Ellen open the window and you thought you heard a door bang?"

"Yes."

"Do you think what you heard could have been a car door?"

She shook her head, "Kaye, I've been over this again and again--with you, the police and fire investigators, and in my own mind. I'm not even sure what I heard at this point. But yes, I suppose it could have been a car door."

I sat down on the cot opposite her, took one of her hands and looked intently into her eyes. "Look, Barbara, I know you've been through a lot. We all have. But it's important. I think Mary Ellen must have gone to sleep pretty early that night. Otherwise how could the sleeping pill have taken such a hold on her? But you and Taylor both said you heard her bang the door and open the window about one o'clock. That supports the theory that Mary Ellen was up and may have set the fire."

"Hold on there a minute," Barbara said. "I heard her open the window early on. My kids were still up so it was before nine. The door banging is what I heard at one o'clock."

Something clicked in my mind. If Mary Ellen opened the window before nine, that meant Nicky and her kids left the room soon after. That was pretty much what Nicky told me. The house meeting usually ended before I came on shift at nine, and Nicky said she'd gone to Eileen's room right after the house meeting. But who banged the door if Mary Ellen was asleep?

"Are you sure it was one o'clock when you heard the door bang?"

Barbara's brow wrinkled. She shook her head, splaying her hands palms up. "I'm not sure, Kaye. Eileen was up. She went to bed just after that. Ask her."

Easy to say, but Eileen had gone to the Boulder safe house just after the fire. But maybe I didn't have to ask. Starr had told me Eileen let Starr in. It must have been three o'clock. The bang could have been a car door, or it could have been the noise of someone starting the fire. I hoped and prayed it wasn't Amanda, but it was beginning to look more and more possible.

Taylor came in and threw himself on Barbara's lap. "Mom, I'm hungry," he said. Somehow as he said it, he made himself look as little and as fragile as a baby bird.

Something niggled in my mind. There was something else I should ask about, but I wasn't sure what. Anyway, Barbara needed to feed her kids, and I needed to go home. Time was up. "Thanks, Barbara," I said and went back to the office.

Sonya from the Red Cross relieved me, and I shuffled off to take my kids to see Mo and the baby. It took thirty minutes in late rush hour traffic to get home. Tuna casserole took another thirty minutes to make--ten minutes to eat. No one liked tuna in my house except me. I made it because it was cheap and it was good for them. I tried to hustle then, but Hannah changed clothes twice before we left, and Denver General was across town from my house. We stopped to pick out a magazine and some flowers in the hospital gift shop. So we had only eight minutes left before the end of visiting hours. A red headed nurse was pushing the baby's plastic bassinet out as we entered the dimly lit room.

"Oh no," said Hannah. "Is that Sara?"

The nurse smiled. "I'm taking her to get a bath."

"Can I come?" Hannah asked.

"Me too," said RJ.

"It's up to Mrs. Preston, and your mother," said the nurse. I looked at Mo uncertainly.

"Take notes," she said to my kids. "You'll have to do this when you babysit."

The nurse smiled, and my kids were gone before I could say boo. I sat down in the chair next to the bed, and handed Mo the flowers and magazine.

"Kaye, they're beautiful," she said, sniffing at the flowers.

"Good. How are you feeling?"

"Tired." She set the flowers on the table beside her, leaving the magazine in her lap.

She looked tired. The shadows under her eyes were even worse than they'd been this morning, and all the makeup she'd glopped on looked streaky as though it were melting. Her hair looked uncombed and she wore a hospital gown.

"I'm going to get out of here and let you get to sleep in just a minute. I just want to tell you..." I reached out to take her hand and noticed a huge purple bruise where the sleeve ended on her upper arm.

"My God!" My radar went up. Could Bill be beating her? I'd never seen any sign, but he was so moody. When Mo was admitted, the ER nurse had said I should talk to Bill. I'd thought at the time that sounded weird.

But this was Mo. If anything were wrong, she'd tell me. We'd always been close. Since the day she was born, and my sister had laid her in my skinny eight-year-old arms, there'd been a connection beyond that of aunt and niece. If there were a problem, Mo would tell me.

"What?" She followed my gaze to the bruise. "Oh, they couldn't get the IV in."

"That must have hurt." It didn't look like a place that would bruise when they put an IV in, but I knew it was hard to hit Mo's veins.

"I was thinking about other things at the time."

Probably true. "You mean labor hurt more than that?" I traced the bruise with the tip of my finger. Mo had a theory mothers exaggerated their labor pains to the childless.

"Just a bit."

I smiled, stood up and hugged her. "Mo, I just wanted to tell you. She's beautiful. You and Bill did good."

Her eyes glittered with tears. "I think so too."

"Where is Bill anyway? Sleeping?"

"It was a long night," she said.

She sure wasn't talking much. "I guess so. Get some sleep. I'm going to get Hannah and RJ and collapse myself." I walked back toward the door.

"Everything okay?" she asked.

I turned back toward the bed and wrinkled my nose. "We're going back to Beginnings tomorrow."

"Are you okay with that?"

"I'll let you know later when I see how it all turns out." I paused, reluctant to bring the subject up when Mo just had the baby, but needing to know. "You told me Honecker came to the emergency room when Mary Ellen came in?"

"The skinny guy with the skunk hairdo?"

That was one way to describe him. I nodded.

"Yes, I told you--he was nutso." Mo sounded sleepy, and I felt guilty.

"I just wondered how he and the mom got there so fast. We didn't know who to notify because we couldn't get to the files inside the shelter, and Mary Ellen was unconscious."

"Maybe the husband?" Mo shrugged, "I don't know. I told you, Mary Ellen wasn't my patient."

"When do you get out of here?" I stood at the door now, really about to leave.

"Tomorrow."

"That's great. So we'll see you in a week or so when you're settled down?" She nodded.

"Sure you don't want a cook or a diaper changer over there earlier?"

Mo smiled, "As I remember it, you hate changing diapers."

"I was thinking of my kids, not me."

I left the room on her laugh, collecting my kids on the way to the elevator.

I stayed at home with them long enough to tell them to do their homework, and then I went back out the door again--feeling guilty because I didn't spend more time with them. Guilt seemed to be my middle name these days.

But I had to catch up with Mary Ellen's husband Harry, and this was the only time I had to do it.

He opened the door to his small neat stucco home as though visitors at ten o'clock at night were routine. His white shirt was half unbuttoned, his thinning dark hair mussed, and I saw a woman on the couch behind him in a black negligee that contrasted oddly with the prissy Victorian furnishings of the room. He followed my line of sight and pulled the door behind him, forcing me out a little further on the dark front stoop.

"Hi, I'm Kaye Berreano from Beginnings," I said awkwardly, not knowing what to say now. I'd gotten what I came for already. Olivia told me the truth. Harry had a girlfriend, and from the slight tummy I'd seen under that negligee, she was pregnant. Worse, he'd already established her in Mary

Ellen's house. Still I had to say something. "I met you at the funeral. I need to talk to you about Mary Ellen."

The corner of Harry's mustached mouth tipped up in amusement as though he'd caught me in the middle of something instead of the other way around. "What can I do for you, Mrs. Berreano?"

"It's Ms."

Harry nodded, still smiling and urbane. "I wondered if you knew..." How I was going to complete the sentence I had no idea, when inspiration suddenly struck. "How did your mother-in law and Reverend Honecker get notified the night of the fire?"

Harry looked nonplussed; he evidently expected me to say something about the girlfriend. But what was there to say? I'd done the best I could by catching him in the act. Harry wouldn't tell me anything he hadn't told the police, and he wasn't so dumb that he'd incriminate himself anyway. He must have known the husband was always suspect in a case of suspicious death. But maybe I could rule out Honecker.

Harry shook his head, bewildered. "You'd have to ask them, I suppose. They told me."

Say what? "Didn't someone from the Emergency room call you?"

"No. I first learned about Mary Ellen when Ethel called from the Emergency Room."

***

The next morning the phone rang before I even got the kids off to school. I approached it as warily as I would a snake. Early morning calls were usually something I'd rather not know.

"Katherine?" It was my mother of course. No one but my mother calls me Katherine. No one but my mother would dare.

"Hi, Mom."

"Where is Maureen?"

Had I just been thinking my mother was safe from Alzheimer's? Maybe not. "Mo's in the hospital. She just had the baby."

"You mean she hasn't gone to you? I felt sure she would. Where is she?"

I wasn't used to hearing my mother sound so shaken. Her voice reminded me that she was, after all, a very old lady. "Mom, what are you talking about? I went to the hospital last night. I saw her. Mo's in Denver General. She's fine. She had a beautiful baby girl."

"I just got off the phone with your sister. She tried to call Mo this morning to talk about her plans to visit and help with the baby. It is Patty's grandchild after all. But when she called the hospital, they told her Mo had checked out. And there's no answer at the apartment. Mo must be trying to hide from that husband of hers. Your sister is hysterical."

My mother's voice told me my sister's hysteria was my fault because I should know what was happening with Mo. I put that aside to deal with later. There were other things to consider now.

"Why would she hide from Bill?" But I knew. I remembered his absence from the hospital, the bruise on Mo's arm, the heavy makeup, and the early check-in time to the hospital. I knew Bill beat Mo. And Mo hadn't told me.

The line was silent, but I knew my mother was crying. There were no sniffing or sobbing sounds. I'd never seen my mother cry, but I knew she was now.

"Mom, I'll find her, I promise. It'll be all right. I'll find her."

I got off the phone with an ache in my chest. Somehow, I managed to send the kids off to school without them guessing something was wrong. The minute they went out the door, I got on the phone.

I called Denver General. Mo had definitely checked out. I called Mo and Bill's apartment--no answer. Then I called every safe house in Northern Colorado, using my status as a safe house counselor to get information they would give no one else. Mo wasn't at any of them.

Chapter 16

It must have been nine o'clock before I realized that I was due in court that morning for my divorce. I threw on my good red suit, ran a brush through my hair, and rushed out the door. Lucky for me, Merv had done his job. I didn't have to think about the divorce at all. It was a done deal. Considering my state of mind, that was good.

No one mentioned how or why, but the settlement had become much more equitable. Without a murmur, the court awarded me custody of the kids, the Volvo and the mountain cabin, not to mention half the here-to-fore hidden bank account, and various articles of furniture including the family room suite I liked so much. There was also a little protection against an unstable economy that I liked. The child support rose with the inflation index each year. I didn't have to even mouth the letters IRS to Roger. Merv and Art arranged it all.

Roger sat on the other side of the room in his black Armani suit, regarding me sullenly. I hoped that Merv had not been too heavy-handed with my threat to report Roger's little transgressions to the tax hotline. Not that I felt guilty--not at all. He should have been a little less creative in his accounting for his clients. In the future, I was sure he would be. This was not a threat I could use again. But all I wanted was what was fair for the kids-- and me. He got the half-million-dollar Green Mountain house, half of the money and most of the furniture. I wasn't out to scalp him with my threats.

When I thought about it, I felt sure the threats were unnecessary anyway. Roger wanted to do right by his kids. That, said the lawyers, was what we all wanted.

It seemed like an anti-climax. We signed the papers, and that was it. The money would be transferred that day. The car was mine as soon as I wanted. I could take delivery on the furniture immediately.

Needless to say, I traded cars with Roger right then and there.

I should have been happy, but I just wanted to get out of there. Satisfactory as it was, my mind wasn't even on my divorce as I went to work. As the Volvo ate the miles between the courthouse and the safe house, I desperately tried to figure out who else I could call to find out where Mo had gone. I was so preoccupied that I almost pulled into the lot at the Red Cross shelter, when I realized that it was moving day. It was our first day back at Beginnings. Liz and Brett would help the residents actually move, they wanted me to man the phones. I zipped over to the safe house parking lot and almost ran over Liz and Amanda in the process. They were unloading what looked to be a heavy trunk. Liz wore a heavy, cream-colored sweater embroidered with flowers, over her black pants. But still she had to be cold, since the day was frigid. Icy spots lined the sidewalk from yesterday's storm.

Not the best day to move.

Amanda had dressed more sensibly. Her lithe figure was bundled in a blue barn coat, and she'd covered her head with a navy knit cap.

I got out of the car and called, "Hey, is there anything you want me to help move over here?"

Liz said, "In that car? Kaye, I don't want to even breathe on it. "

I smiled. "Need a hand?" I gestured to the trunk.

"If you could get the door," Amanda said.

I ran to get in front of them and undid the spring on the storm door, holding the heavy wooden door open with my foot.

As they lugged the trunk past me, Liz said, "I take it the court settlement is over."

"Yes. You see before you an official divorcee."

She and Amanda set their burden down in a corner of the service porch. Amanda rolled her shoulders as though they were stiff, and went back out to finish unloading.

Liz stopped in front of me and cocked a sandy eyebrow. She motioned toward the Volvo. "It looks like you did okay."

"Not too bad."

She beamed. "Good for you. I knew you wouldn't let him get away with everything." She patted me on the shoulder, and started to follow Amanda.

"Liz," I said it quietly, but my throat ached with the need to cry.

She turned back to me and scanned my face.

"My niece left her husband. It looks like he beat her."

"She didn't come to you?"

I shook my head. Tears scalded my eyes.

"I'm sorry." She reached out and put her hand on my arm. "Is there anything I can do?"

"Pray for her, will you?"

She nodded, and I walked slowly into the house.

I'd gotten halfway to the office when I realized who I should call. Sheena, the tall black ER nurse who had first told me Mo was in the hospital; she would know where Mo was now. I felt sure of it.

I dialed the number at Denver General feeling hopeful for the first time all day. Sheena Stamford, please.

"She's not in right now. Can I help you?"

"Actually no, I really need to talk to her."

"She works three to eleven," said the nasal-voiced clerk.

"Could you give me her home number? I am Maureen Preston's aunt, and this is very important."

"No, I'm sorry. I can't give out that information."

It would have to wait until she came on shift at the hospital that night. Meanwhile, I needed to get to work.

One thing about Beginnings, it took my mind off myself. It wasn't because of the daytime commotion either, because there wasn't any. Amanda and Liz unloaded Liz's car and that was it for about an hour. No phones, no people tramping in and out, nothing. It felt spooky. I would have sworn I smelled smoke from the fire even over the fresh coat of paint. It was cold, and I didn't want to take my coat off or sit down. So I wandered from room to room, aimlessly. That's when I ran into Brett in the upstairs hall. I jumped as though I'd met Mary Ellen's ghost.

Brett peered at me over the top of a stack of boxes. Her short red hair stuck straight out from under her knit cap. She left a trail of wet spots on the flowered carpet behind her where she had tracked in snow. "You okay? I didn't mean to scare you."

I took a deep breath and told my heart to cut it out with the thumping. "I'm okay. When is everybody going to get here?"

"What everybody? Half of them are moving out."

"Really? Who?"

Brett set her boxes on a small table, but it wobbled under the weight. With a shake of her head, she picked them back up, steadying the table with her foot. "Starr--you knew about Starr, right?"

"Uh huh."

"Then there's Cindy, and uh--what's her name--the quiet one?"

"Naomi?"

"That's her." Brett moved into the front bedroom and stacked the boxes on the bottom bunk bed.

"When did all this happen?"

"Cindy left last night--went to stay with her mother. Naomi's leaving this morning. She's going to share an apartment with a friend. I don't think either one of them wanted to come back here." She shrugged. "Bad memories. You can't blame them."

I didn't blame them. But I couldn't help wondering whether memories or fear motivated them.

The door banged downstairs, and I heard a child screech. I left Brett to the boxes and went down to see what was going on.

Barbara stood by the front door, her hands full of suitcases, hanging clothes slung over her shoulder. Taylor clung to her blue jeaned leg.

Zeke hitched up sagging jeans and chased Daria out the door as I reached the bottom step. Barbara shouted, "Settle down you two."

"You've got your hands full," I said, reaching out for the hangers.

She sighed, relieved to have a more manageable burden. "I can't believe how much stuff we've accumulated."

"It all adds up," I said.

She eased Taylor gently off her leg. "Go find Zeke, honey. I'm going to take this stuff upstairs."

Taylor stuck his bottom lip out, the word no already forming, when Zeke stuck his head in the door. "Taylor, come look. I found the coolest snake hole."

Taylor ran out as I was still shaking my head. "It's January; there are no snakes around that I know of."

Barbara shrugged. "So much the better. They can poke around to their heart's content and not get hurt."

As I trailed her slowly up the stairs, holding the hangers high so as not to drag her neatly pressed suits, I thought of something I hadn't asked the night before.

"Barbara, you said Eileen stayed up late the night of the fire, but what about Nicky?"

"What about Nicky?" She grunted, trying to kick the bedroom door open with her foot.

I scooted around her, shifting clothes as I did, so I could open the door. Although I'd already checked out the house, the unfamiliarly neat bedroom still startled me. Our volunteers had worked overtime cleaning and fixing up the rooms while we were gone. The result looked better than anything I'd seen since I had come to work here. Of course it was nothing the women, their kids and all of their belongings wouldn't change as soon as they hit the place.

"Did Nicky go to sleep early that night?"

Barbara flung her haul onto the bed. I thought I caught a glimpse of uneasiness.

"Nicky said she and the kids slept in your room that night." I prodded.

Barbara's face cleared. "They did, but I didn't know if I should tell you or not. I didn't want to get her in trouble."

I frowned. Changing rooms wasn't a big deal. "You mean because she was fighting with Mary Ellen?"

"Yes. But Nicky didn't leave the room all night. She slept at the foot of my bed like a dog from about ten on."

"So she wasn't a part of the plan to sneak Starr in?"

Barbara shook her head. "I don't think she even knew Starr left. But I know for sure, Nicky didn't get up to let Starr in. She slept hard. Nothing, not the kids, not Eileen moving in and out--nothing until the fire alarm woke her. Then I was glad she slept there, because she helped me get my kids out."

I hung Barbara's clothes in her closet and wandered back downstairs. She was busy. Besides I'd already asked all the questions I could think of. This Nancy Drew routine did not come naturally to me.

The house still felt peculiar and empty even with the Washburn kids running in and out. I decided to be pragmatic. If the house felt odd, it was probably because it was so chilly. I went to the thermostat and blasted our budget by pointing the needle towards eighty. Then I went to the office to see if I could talk to Mo's friend Sheena.

This time at least, the clerk--a Southerner by the sound of her-- confirmed that she'd come in. "She says she can't talk to you right now."

I didn't care who I kissed up to. I had to find Mo. "This is very important," I pleaded.

"I'm sorry."

Maybe they have better manners down South, but the woman sounded sincere. Don't ask me why I picked that moment to get stubborn. "I'll just come down then. Maybe then she'll have time to talk to me."

I heard a hurried, whispered conversation, then Sheena's voice came on. "I've got it, thanks, Rhea."

I decided to proceed as though I didn't know Sheena didn't want to talk to me. I waited a moment until I heard the sound of the other extension being hung up. "Sheena? This is Kaye Berreano, Mo's aunt."

"Yes?" Sheena's voice sounded bored.

"She and the baby checked out today, and I'm concerned about her. I hoped you could tell me if you've heard from her."

"No, actually, I haven't heard a word." I didn't know Sheena well at all, but her voice reminded me of Hannah's when I've caught her doing something she knows she shouldn't. The only way I can describe it is as a sort of high pitched gulp as in, "Who, me?"

"Sheena." I let my voice get quietly serious. "Is Bill beating her?"

"Why don't you ask him?"

"I haven't been able to locate him either." Besides, her reply answered the question for me.

"I can't help you there." Her voice said she took a certain satisfaction from the fact. Did that mean she knew where both Bill and Mo were?

"Look, Sheena, my whole family is in an uproar. My seventy-nine-year-old mother called me this morning crying. My sister, Mo's mother, is hysterical, and I haven't been able to concentrate all day. Now I need to know where she is. Please if you know, please, please tell me."

"I can't tell you." Sheena's voice matched mine for seriousness now. I had to believe her. "I know she wouldn't want you or her mom or her grandmother to worry. But I promised her I wouldn't tell anyone. All I can say is that she's safe, and that she's doing a lot of thinking."

"Why?" I wailed. My sister wasn't the only hysterical one in the family. "Does she think I'd tell Bill? Because she should know that I'd never ever even think of it."

"She does know that," Sheena said. "She told me if you knew, you wouldn't stop until she left him. She wants to make sure for herself that whatever she does, it's right for her and for the baby."

"So he is beating her."

"I already said more than I should have, but I don't want you or your family worrying anymore. Mo's safe."

"But where? I need to see for myself."

"Mo's safe." Sheena repeated. "She just needs some time to think."

And with that, it seemed, I would have to be satisfied. Sheena hung up.

The rest of the day passed in a haze. When it was over, I dragged myself home and tried to call my mother. She wasn't home, but Hannah overheard me leaving a message and told RJ. So by the time I got off the phone, RJ was ready to go over to his cousin's apartment and beat Bill up. Hannah was crying.

"Look, kids, I don't know for sure what's going on. Let's not lose our heads." I sat at the kitchen table trying to hold them both with my eyes.

"He's really hitting her?" Hannah asked.

I nodded. "It looks that way."

"I'll kill him," RJ said.

"No, you won't," I said firmly. "That's not the way to handle this."

"It's the way he handled this," RJ said.

"So you want to stoop to his level?" My voice reminded me of my mother's. I wasn't sure I liked that. Something in me wanted to punish Bill as much as RJ did, and the old "won't stoop to his level" argument just didn't sound convincing.

"I want to make him feel the same way he made Mo feel," RJ said.

Yes. He'd said it exactly right. I felt the same way. I'd counseled women and families to take the legal remedies available to them, but when it got up close and personal, I wanted revenge, too.

"RJ, that won't help Mo. She's the one we have to think of now."

"But we don't know where she is," Hannah sobbed.

"But we know she's safe, and she's thinking about all this. We have to be available to help her do whatever she needs done."

RJ nodded, looking somehow older than he had when the conversation started. "I'm here, and I'll do anything she wants--anything she'll let me do."

* * *

The phone rang late that night. I raced to it, my white nightgown flying out in back of me, hoping against hope that it was Mo.

It wasn't, of course.

"Hope you're happy, Kaye. Got what you wanted." The voice was Roger's, but he sounded funny. He slurred the words together.

Was he drunk? I hadn't seen him drunk in years. He was much too stuffy-careful for that.

"If you mean the divorce, Roger, I think it must have been what you wanted too, or else you wouldn't have been playing around." It was too late at night to take this kind of garbage. How dare he call me when he was drunk?

"What're you doing home anyway? Now we're divorced, you quit that stinkin' job at the safe house?"

"Roger, I told you that I changed shifts to be home with the kids at night. What is it you called for anyway?"

"Wanted to speak to you. Wanted to tell you. Should have known."

"Roger, if you can't get to the point, I'm going to hang up."

He muttered to himself then, something about women. I couldn't catch it all.

Louder he said, "Safe house always did mean more to you than your own family. S'a shame the damn thing didn't burn down to the ground." Then with a bang, he hung up.

Chapter 17

It wouldn't have been an exaggeration to say I stayed up all night worrying. I couldn't help asking myself if Roger burned the safe house. I still couldn't fit all the pieces together. I knew only one thing for sure. This had stopped being about Mary Ellen, or even my need for a full-time job. I felt sad over Mary Ellen's death. Somehow it should have been prevented, but it hadn't been. But I knew that nothing I had done could have prevented it.

I took this personally now. For safety's sake, for the remaining residents' sakes, I needed to find the arsonist, even if he was my children's father.

When I finally did get to sleep, I slept heavily. The next thing I knew, Hannah was banging on the door. "Mom, aren't you up yet? Don't you want to see our report cards?"

"You guys are back already? I didn't even hear you come in."

"You didn't hear us leave either," Hannah said. "And we came back late 'cause RJ had to show everybody on the bus his report card. I was sick of it, so I came home without him."

I nodded; they never walked back from the bus together anyway. That wouldn't be cool. But if RJ was showing off his report card, that was wonderful. It must mean he got a good one. Sure enough, RJ's grades were up.

Promising to really celebrate this weekend, I made some hamburgers for dinner, ate with the kids and got ready for work.

I was actually at the door when the phone rang.

Hannah answered. "It's Grandmom," she yelled the words to me from the kitchen.

"Katherine?"

"Mom, I would have called, but I don't know any more about Mo than I did Thursday."

"She's here." My mother's voice sounded tense.

"In New Jersey? So she's at Patty's?"

My sister lived forty minutes away from Mom.

"No. She's here with me."

Why didn't Mo go to her own parents instead of her grandmother?

"She just showed up at the door with the baby in her arms. She looks terrible. She's so thin, you'd never know she just had a baby. She hasn't said much, either."

"But she's okay?"

"As well as can be expected," said Mom. "I wish she would talk to us."

"I guess she will when she's ready." It sounded and felt lame, but I couldn't think of anything else to say. If I knew my mother at all, she wanted to take Mo in her arms and make it all better. But she couldn't, and neither could I.

"Tell her," I paused. "Tell her I'll miss her, Mom."

I told the kids the news and was rewarded with their relieved smiles. But I had no time to rejoice. If traffic was against me, I was going to be late for work.

* * *

I came in the back door, since it was the closest to the parking lot. I walked through the darkened house, room by room, amazed at the transformation from the cold empty house it had been when I last saw it. Someone had gotten all the stuff off the service porch. Even the plants were back in place on the window sills in there. We had a few boxes to put away in the kitchen, mostly canned goods. But the kitchen sink was full of dinner dishes. The bathroom already reeked of mildew again. Essentially, Beginnings looked as though we'd never left.

I was glad I'd gotten back to my nine to five-thirty shift, even if just for the night. My body felt in tune with the time, and I knew the sets of problems the shift encountered. I already knew that I would have to get on Nicky's back to wash those dishes. It was her turn for KP. Best of all, I didn't have to worry about another counselor encountering the arsonist.

The living room felt over-crowded with Amanda, Nicky, Barbara, and Kirsten Birkhoffer from Legal Aid. We held a legal clinic night every other Friday, and Kirsten, a small, genuine blonde with the pale complexion and eyelashes to match, handled the meetings with energy and compassion.

There was one thing I couldn't figure out. Liz didn't have to conduct this meeting, so she should have been long gone. Yet she was still here.

Nicky's kids chased Barbara's younger ones around the room although all the kids should have been settled in their rooms for the house meeting. Their mothers ignored them, and with all the woman talking, the noise level rose to a nerve damaging level. But Kirsten knew how to deal with all that.

So why was Liz still here?

"Hello, hello, hello, everyone," I called. I took off my coat and headed toward the office.

Liz followed.

And that made me nervous. Did she have something she needed to tell me in private? Something bad?

"Guess what?" She practically sang the words.

Her tone dispelled my fears. What I had taken for tension must have been something else. I smiled at her. "From the sound of your voice, Beginnings must have won the lottery."

She laughed and waved a white envelope in my face. "I don't know about Beginnings. But the checks are in. They did a special check cut since they messed them up so badly."

"Thank God. Oh, so I won the lottery?"

She waved her hand in a circular motion. "Just open it," she said.

The amount on the check made me raise my eyebrows. "I think accounting is still screwed up."

She shook her head, smiling broadly and moved out the office door back towards the meeting. "Nope. You got a raise. I put you in for one weeks ago, and I didn't want to tell you until it was approved. They got it just in time for the last check--which was the good news. The bad news was accounting's problems included the raise as well as the insurance."

I smiled. "So, can I run and cash this before someone changes their mind?"

"Actually Kaye, I hope you don't mind, but now that you're here, I'm going to hustle. Carl and I are going to the movies," Liz said. "The report is on the desk."

I waved to show that was all right with me, and walked back toward the office. I hung my coat on the hook behind the door, took Liz's off her hook and went back out, handing it to her silently.

Liz laughed. "In other words, get out of here already."

Barbara said, "At least she didn't tell you straight out."

"Now I'm not usually that rude, am I?" I asked, smiling.

"You're not shy about letting people know how you feel, Kaye," Amanda chimed in.

"Geez, this is the last time I'll try to do something nice for somebody."

"Oh Kaye, you're always nice," Liz said in a soothing voice, winking widely to the residents over my shoulder as she shrugged into her coat. Then in a stage-whisper she said, "There's no point in getting that temper of hers riled up. You guys have to live with her tonight."

I picked up a paper from the table and threw it at her. She laughed and ducked out the front door.

Kirsten said, "Since you're so anxious to get rid of us, Kaye, I'll leave you alone with your residents. I just wanted to help Amanda here finish filling out this form."

"Finish whatever you want, Kirsten. I've got all night."

"Yeah, you have to stay, Kirsten, please," said Nicky. "She won't bug me to do the dishes until you leave."

"Thanks, ladies, I appreciate your hospitality," said Kirsten, as she rose and gathered her papers. "But I'm sure that my family wants to see me tonight."

Kirsten left with a quiet click of the door latch that resonated in my ears.

"Well," Barbara said, clearing her throat. "I'm going to get these kids to bed. It's nine o'clock."

"Aaah, Mom," said Daria. "Bud and Jena are staying up, and they're little kids."

"We are not little," said Bud.

"Jena and Bud are not staying up," said Nicky. She swooped down and picked up her daughter. "They're going to bed right now."

Jena opened her big brown eyes wide, and shook her head at her mother, but Nicky looked her straight in the eyes, and nodded solemnly. With her little pink mouth pursed in resignation, Jena nodded back.

With one hand on Bud, still carrying Jena, Nicky looked back at me as she went out of the room. "Just a sec, Kaye, I promise. Then I'll come back to do those dishes."

Barbara followed with her three in tow. Absentmindedly, I wandered into the office to get the day's report. I heard a male voice say, "Just wait until you get a look at this one."

My heart thumped heavily. Then I realized, Liz had left the radio in the office on. "This snow is promising to shut down..."

The mother and kid parade sounded like elephants on the stairs, drowning out the radio announcer's voice. I heard one of the Washburn kids yelp briefly, a door slammed; the house quieted down again.

"...across the whole front range," said the radio announcer's voice. "This is the best..."

I clicked it off.

When I came back out to the living room, the room was empty. Amanda must have left while my attention was elsewhere.

The house felt so quiet, I heard the ticking of the ugly metallic sunburst clock on the wall behind the couch. The cozy pools of light formed by the lamps seemed dwarfed by shadows. I quickly turned on the overhead lights, and then noticed that all the windows glared back at me like black gaping holes. I walked quickly around the cold room, telling myself that pulling down the shades would help keep the room's warmth in.

One hand on the shade, I glanced outside anxiously. The view held my eyes. Just since I'd come in, the scene outside had changed. Snow swirled crazily, whipped by a vicious wind which bent tree branches and whistled at the windows. Already, we had some accumulation, reflecting light, making the night look almost moonlit. As I pulled down the last shade, I thought I saw something move on the porch just beyond the window.

Only the snow falling, I told myself. Even so I turned on the porch light and peered through the glass for some kind of repetition of the movement.

"What do you see, Kaye?" Barbara's voice startled me, but she seemed not to notice. "Oh, is it snowing again? I was hoping we were going to get a break."

"Not tonight," I said as I pulled the shade down. "Did you get your kids tucked in?"

"I think so. They were pretty tired from the move anyway. I'm pretty tired myself. I thought I'd make some hot cocoa and get to bed."

"Good, you can keep me company while I do those dishes," said Nicky, bounding briefly through the room on her way to the kitchen.

I followed her, hoping for some fresh coffee. Barbara trailed.

"Where's Amanda?" I asked.

Nicky jerked a thumb at her former bedroom, the room she'd shared with Mary Ellen behind the kitchen. "Isn't that weird?" she asked. "I couldn't believe it when she said she wanted to sleep there. You couldn't pay me to stay there." She turned the water on full force, and scoured vigorously at one of the dirty pans stacked there.

It wouldn't be my first choice either. "I thought we were going to keep that room closed."

Nicky shrugged. "Liz tried. She told Amanda that it wasn't done yet, but Amanda just about cried to get it. So then Liz said that the workmen could work around her."

"Did Amanda say why she wanted it?" I asked, crowding in beside her to check out the coffee pot. At least it felt warm.

Nicky shook her head. "Not to me she didn't." She looked over her shoulder at Barbara, who also shook her head no.

"This whole place gives me the creeps," Nicky said. "I want to get out of here so bad, I'm thinking of going back home."

That surprised me and I didn't know why. We got women who bounced back and forth like ping pong balls between the safe house and home. Yet Nicky's situation, and her still-purple scars, made the idea seem impossible. I'd done her intake interview. Her description of the scene that had made her leave home was all the more horrendous because she told it so matter-of-factly.

I didn't feel so accepting. I couldn't get the image of her boyfriend holding a knife to her pregnant belly out of my mind for the longest time. I didn't know why she didn't miscarry then.

"You don't mean that," I said.

My thoughts must have been evident on my face, because Nicky gave me a strangely defensive look. Then she said, "Least he never tried to burn me to death." Her thumb hit the spray handle, releasing a torrent that resonated on the pot, making talking impossible for a moment. She reached for the next dish with her right hand, as she put the pot on the counter with the other.

"You sure about that?" Amanda, in plaid pajamas that looked as though she had borrowed them from her husband's drawer, walked to the table with a glass of water in her hand.

I looked up in the middle of pouring myself a cup of coffee. "What do you mean?"

"If you ask me, any one of our men could have been dumb enough to pull this stunt," Amanda said.

"So how did he find us?" I asked.

Nicky wagged her head furiously. "My Sam didn't do it. He doesn't even know where this place is."

Roger did. I shook my head. There was no evidence that anybody else was near the house. Did Amanda realize that I didn't quite trust her anymore? Maybe she was trying to deflect my suspicions.

"I'm tired of thinking about it," said Nicky, wringing out a wash cloth. "At least at home, I've only got to share a room with Sam. The kids got their own rooms, and I got somebody to help take care of them. I don't have to do it all myself."

"Does he help take care of the kids?" Barbara looked interested, as though that were a new concept.

Nicky nodded. "Oh yeah." She didn't look around from wiping the stove. "He changes diapers, feeds 'em--you know, canned spaghetti and stuff like that. He's pretty good with them."

"My husband would never do that." Barbara's voice showed she was impressed. She took a sip of her cocoa. "He'd tell people--'oh yes, I change diapers', but when it came around to doing it..." She shook her head. "It was always my turn."

Nicky said, "Guess that's why you haven't gone back, huh? I mean, you making so much money and all, if he doesn't even help out with the kids, who needs him?"

"I'd go home in a minute, but he won't have me." Barbara bit her lip and blinked rapidly to hold back the tears. "He's got some young thing now."

I knew what that felt like.

"Men!" said Amanda.

"Hey, George is all right, isn't he?" I liked the guy myself.

"Yes. He's got some funny ideas, but he's okay."

"So you'd go back if you could?" asked Nicky.

"I'd do anything to get out of this place," Amanda said.

Really? That could account for why she'd been acting so weird. They all were scared, and what could I say? I was scared myself. Nicky hung up her washcloth and went to bed. Barbara and Amanda sipped their drinks in silence before they too slipped away.

I went back through the living room, turning off lights. I'd been silly before. Lights wouldn't make a difference one way or another. A boom box blared from the downstairs bedroom, then quickly the volume was turned down.

Just as I walked into the office, the phone rang. My stomach turned, just as though I knew who was on the other end.

"Beginnings," I answered.

"Now, Kaye, I told you to get those ladies out of there." His voice sounded tantalizingly familiar, patronizing and maddening. I wanted to reach through the phone line and strangle the creep.

"You don't have much time now."

Chapter 18

That deep voice couldn't be Amanda. Besides, she'd just turned down the music in her room. My mind flipped into over drive, but my thinking stayed very, very clear.

A man had made this phone call. So it couldn't be Amanda. Or Roger. I'd know Roger's voice in an instant. He wouldn't sound just hauntingly familiar, he'd be instantly identifiable. Funny, I hadn't thought of these things before. So scratch Roger, and Amanda, but since the voice was male, it had to be an outsider--despite the evidence.

What about Mary Ellen's husband--handsome Harry? Or Honecker; Mo had told me to watch out for him. Fanatics could do anything in the name of their cause. He knew his way to the safe house. Even Bill suddenly looked like a likely prospect. If he could beat up Maureen, he wouldn't be happy with a shelter for battered women, would he?

I cursed the jerk, whoever he was, for putting these women through this as I dialed 911, then I heard a scratchy sound outside the window.

I got up to check it out. It was a good thing too, because I had walked only halfway around the desk when the window shattered and the chair burst into flames. I spun around, catching sight of a face outside the shattered window. The fire alarm went off just as I screamed with all of my might.

I snatched up the piece of Colorado marble that Liz used as a paper weight from the desk. As a weapon against an armed assailant, it would be useless, but I couldn't think of anything else better to use. I couldn't think at all--except for one thing--I wanted to catch this miserable piece of garbage.

Women's voices filled the house as I dashed for the door. A crowd of nightgowned figures clustered by the stairs.

"Everything is going to be okay. But I could use a little help, Nicky," I picked her name out of the air. "There's a fire in the office."

Instead of the rapid response I'd hoped for, she stood motionless, arms at her sides, mouth open. I suddenly realized that she was afraid, but I couldn't help her right now.

I couldn't stop. I had to get this guy. I called over my shoulder, "It'll be all right. This is just a small fire. Barbara, call the fire department and grab the extinguisher from the hall." Out of the corner of my eye, as I went out, I saw Barbara heading for the office. Nicky ran back up the stairs, and Amanda grabbed a coat to follow me.

Outside the icy air caught at my lungs. Snow swirled and sparkled around the streetlight. No sign of the arsonist. It was so quiet. Snow stung my face, and slid down my collar. Without hesitation, I headed for the parking lot at the side of the house, adrenaline making me fast.

Sure enough, I saw a hooded figure getting in a car with one headlight out. "We must fight the feminists and secular humanists who are breaking up Christian homes," he screamed as he shut the door.

Honecker. Had to be. He knew where this place was.

Cursing, I launched myself at the car, trying to drag him out by his hood. He wasn't that big, but then neither was I. He twisted away from me and pushed me out of the car, his hands bruising me. I dropped my paperweight, but I wouldn't let go of him, even though I fell to the ground. I pulled him down on top of me.

As I did, something fell out of the car next to us. I twisted my head quickly, hoping against hope it wasn't a weapon he was going to use on me. It dawned on me that chasing after this guy wasn't the swiftest thing I'd ever done. No, not a gun--a cell phone chirped and flashed in the snow by my head. That explained how he threw the incendiary device in the window so soon after he called.

With that, I got hot all over again. I wanted to grind the phone under my heel. I wanted to grind him under my heel. I swung a hard punch into his stomach, but though he grunted, he didn't move off me.

Amanda ran up, breathing hard, her heels crunching gravel under the snow. She straddled him as I tried to beat him into submission with Liz's rock. He tried to roll away from us--his mistake. He rolled just enough for me to get out from under him and add my weight to Amanda's on top. "How could you do this, you stupid jerk?" I shook him so hard, his head banged on the snow-covered gravel.

"Stop, Kaye," Amanda's voice sounded shaky. "The police are on their way." She helped me up, dusting snow off my legs and sweater while I carefully kept one booted foot on my prisoner. She directed a vicious kick at my captive. "George, I told you to stay away from here."

George?

Suddenly Amanda was down on the ground, rolling around in the swirling snow, pulling George's hair and gouging him with her finger nails.

"This is her fault," he gasped. "She wouldn't send you home." He struggled to hold her hands still and glared at me, over her; his eyes narrowed, his usually pleasant face a mask of anger. "What does it take, Kaye? You saw us together, you knew there was no reason for Amanda to be here. And I called and warned you. You made me do this. I told you these women need to be home with their husbands."

Amanda bit his hand so hard I saw him start bleeding.

Luckily for George, two squad cars, lights spinning brightly against the night, pulled up soon after. I had no urge to rescue him from his wife, though I knew I should. The way I saw it, they deserved each other--especially since she obviously knew he'd been the arsonist.

Four uniformed cops spilled out of the cars and wasted no time pulling the two apart. "What's going on here?" said the older balding cop, hanging back a bit from his colleagues.

"This man just threw an incendiary into the battered women's shelter here." I waved my hand back toward Beginnings. "I'm pretty sure George here is the one who set the fire we had awhile back, too. Lieutenant Farrell has been in charge of that investigation."

The bald cop nodded and spoke into the radio.

One of the younger cops, holding a struggling Amanda, spoke. "So he threw something in the safe house, and you sicced her on him?"

"Actually," I drawled, looking at Amanda's angry red face, while connecting her desire to have the downstairs room with her comment about how she'd told him to stay away, "She's his wife. And I think she knew he was the arsonist, yet did nothing."

The young cop's eyes widened, but the other cops nodded. They divided up. Two cops took Amanda back into Beginnings to talk, while two cops stayed with George.

Meanwhile, a fire truck rolled up in front of the house, its lights and sirens splitting the night.

I rushed back to the house.

Inside, Nicky stood dressed in her coat, arms full of black garbage bags packed with clothes. At her side, both kids cried and clung to her. The

Washburn kids, headed by twelve- year-old Zeke, stood in front of her, trying to talk her out of something.

I wanted to talk to her. Needed to. But the fire...

Beyond her, I saw Barbara in the office, gesturing to the firemen. I shook my head. Barbara looked like she was handling it well. Nicky was the first priority.

I held out my hand and took a bag.

"You can't stop me, Kaye," she said. "I'm leaving."

"Nicky, it's over. There won't be any more fires."

She shook her head. "I don't care. I'm going home. I can't take staying here with no crazies no more."

And no matter what I said, that was it. She was going. I helped her take the bags to the car and belted the kids in their car seats with a sinking feeling. Nicky's situation wasn't good. She'd be back. If he didn't kill her first.

The fire truck pulled off just after Nicky did. I didn't bother going back to the safe house. Barbara and those kids were incredible. They didn't need me.

I stood in the parking lot, wishing for a cigarette and waiting for Farrell.

It took a while--but as soon as I saw the lights of the car turn into the lot, I knew it was him. I wasn't prepared for the surge of happiness I felt as I waited for him to get out of the car.

His graying red hair looked ruffled--not quite bed head, but still not as well-groomed as I'd come to expect, and he wore faded jeans instead of the usual dark slacks. As he drew closer, I saw that his blue eyes were shadowed.

"I owe you one," he said.

"How's that?"

He shrugged and smiled at me, his mouth twisted up just a little more on one side than the other. "It looks like you were right all along about Mary Ellen."

I nodded, sudden tears clogging my throat.

"I'm sorry," he said.

By the time the uniformed cops bundled both George and Amanda into a car and left, Farrell had asked me out to coffee.

I hesitated. "My shift's not over yet."

"C'mon, Kaye," He said quietly. "Liz owes you too. If you hadn't insisted on being night counselor tonight, who knows what could have happened? Nobody else believed there was anything to be on guard about."

I shivered at the thought of Dina or Liz caught there in the office when George threw in his incendiary. Did Farrell know that was my nightmare? I looked at him curiously.

He smiled. "She can send someone in to replace you while we talk. Afterall, we need to finish up this case, a-n-d..."

"And?"

"And, I would like to talk to you," he finished.

Of course, I said I would.

Farrell went back to work, getting notes from the cops already there and taking statements from the safe house residents. I simply waited while Liz found a replacement counselor for me. The safe house was a hub of activity with cops swarming over the office and yard again, but the whole feeling in the house was different from earlier in the evening. It was over, and the residents knew it and were relieved.

We ended up at Denney's. The restaurant was crowded with teenagers looking as though they had just come from some concert. Farrell made sure the waitress got us a seat in a booth away from the kids. Then instead of taking the opposite bench, he made me move over, so that he could sit next to me.

I looked around deliberately. "This hardly seems like the place to talk." I let my gaze fall to the small space between us.

Farrell shrugged a little. "I'm sorry. There just aren't that many places open this time of night."

The waitress came up then to take our order. Farrell got cherry pie and some coffee. I ordered decaf.

"So...tell me what you know."

I shrugged. "You've got statements from the whole shelter by now. You know as much as I do."

He waved his hand in a rolling motion. "We'll trade info. Tell me about this George."

Fine, I would go on. "He was the husband of one of our residents. It's kind of complicated. She couldn't just go home if she wanted to, like everyone else. They'd had a big blow-up before she got there and she hurt him so badly he ended up in the hospital. The judge gave her a choice between Beginnings' counseling, and jail."

Farrell nodded as though that made sense. "So George didn't care what he did to get her out."

"No, I don't think it was like that. He really seemed like a nice guy. My guess is he never meant to hurt anybody at first. He just figured that if the safe house were damaged, his wife would have to come home. I bet he was horrified to find out that he'd killed someone-- someone he knew--a member of his church."

"So he's a churchgoer? The guilt must have gotten to him."

I remembered back to Mary Ellen's funeral. No, George didn't seem to feel guilty. He had been angry that day, but I'd thought it was because of Dina. Looking back I could see that it was the whole idea of the shelter itself that made him so upset. Slowly, I said, "He figured Mary Ellen's death had to mean we would send the residents home. But it didn't work out the way he planned. Not only did we not send the women home, we re-opened the safe house. I don't think he figured on that."

The waitress came back with our order.

I accepted my coffee with a smile and took a sip.

But Farrell ignored the pie in front of him, reaching out to touch my arm.

"Kaye, I think we have to accept that it went deeper than that. The responding officer said that George didn't have one good word to say about you. The officer seemed to think George meant to try to hurt you."

I shook my head. "I don't believe that...George..."

Farrell's eyes forced me to look at him. "Believe it. As he saw it, you were the main cause of his trouble. As the counselor working with him and Amanda, he felt you should see they didn't need therapy and send her home."

I swallowed and nodded. "I guess. That's probably true."

He had warned me over and over again on the phone. Yet I still didn't send his wife home. By his logic, there could be only one reason: I wanted to break up his marriage. He'd deliberately lobbed that incendiary at me, and his only regret was that he had missed.

"So let me make sure we've got this all tied up now. As far as you know, he really didn't have anything to do with the woman who died?"

"No, no, he only knew her slightly. I don't know why did he picked her room."

"That I do know." Farrell took some notes from his pocket, tracing down them with his finger until he got to the part he wanted. "He told the responding officer that he saw the window open, and figured it was the laundry room or something." Farrell looked up. "You know better than I do how that place is laid out."

I was silent for a minute thinking about how this fit with what I already knew. But it made a sort of sense. Mary Ellen had opened the window, and George just took the opportunity to set the fire in a metal trash can. "We all made this pretty easy for him."

Farrell nodded grimly. "You counselors really should go over safety procedures at Beginnings. The only real question left is how did George find the safe house in the first place. Isn't the location supposed to be kept secret?"

"He probably just followed his wife back after a joint counseling session. He must have been thinking about doing this for a while," I said slowly.

I realized as I did so, that it had probably been George's figure I saw in Beginnings backyard after the first threatening phone call. "I think he wasn't sure whether or not to really do it. But then he caught his wife and another resident when they went AWOL to visit a bar. That decided it for him. He followed them back, and he got so mad, he decided to start the fire right then and there."

"How awful for his wife," Farrell said. "I know you were pretty ticked at her. Officer York said you thought they deserved one another."

I looked away, letting my gaze roam the restaurant, a little ashamed of my response.

Farrell's calm voice went on. "It wasn't that easy on her though, you know. Turns out, she's known for days. She even warned a couple of residents to leave."

My look around the restaurant reminded of the last time I was here for my counseling session with Amanda and George at Denny's. She must have known then. Had he just told her? That was when her behavior started to become really strange.

I put the thought from my mind. There was nothing I could do. "You said you wanted to talk about something else?"

Farrell reddened. "I know that this is probably not the best moment to do this." He cleared his throat. "But I couldn't say anything before since I was working this case, and I know you are just getting divorced."

"It was final yesterday," I said, fascinated by his color. "Are you asking me for a date?"

"As a matter of fact," he said.

* * *

I went home to Hannah's loud music and RJ snoring on the couch. I shook RJ and sent him to his room to dress for school. I let the music go. Hannah would be gone to school soon. I could put up with it a little.

Besides, I felt like celebrating. But who was there to celebrate with? Dina took over from me at work. Mo was gone. I felt a pang, missing her already.

I could call Roger and tell him I was glad to know the father of my children was not an arsonist. I dialed the number and then hung up before the answering machine ran its course. I didn't say anything. What could I say? There was no message I could leave that he'd understand.

It seemed to be my night for changes--not all of them happy. My hand was still on the phone when it rang again.

Roger sounded hoarse, as though he had just woken up.

"I'll thank you not to call me and bang the phone down in my ear. Do you know what time it is, Kaye?"

"How do you know I did it?" All right, so subtlety wasn't my long suit.

"Hannah's hair-raisers in the background." I laughed. I should have thought of that myself.

"So what was so important that you had to wake me up at six a.m.?"

"You've got a nerve, Roger. At least I had the decency to hang up. You woke me up in the middle of the night with your call, and then I had to listen to your drunken ravings." The words were no sooner out of my mouth than I regretted them. I'd resolved that I would be at least civil with Roger, for the kids' sakes.

"Look, Kaye, I'm really sorry about that." His voice was low and honestly ashamed.

His tone should have made it easier for me to relent, but I couldn't help asking. "Let me guess. You were so upset about having to share half the assets with me that you got bombed, and decided to tell me about it?"

"That wasn't what I called to tell you." I could picture Roger running his hand through his hair as he said this. He sounded embarrassed about the whole thing.

"So?" I prompted.

"So what?"

"What did you call about?" I should have been exasperated with the long stall, but I was intrigued.

"I... I was going to ask you if you'd come back to me."

I laughed, then stopped. "You're not--this is a joke, right?"

"No."

I didn't know what to say except... "What about what's her face?"

"Brenna left me. She and Art Patterson are moving in together."

Whoa. I spared a pang for Art's wife, Lydia. The four of us had spent a lot of time together in the old days. She was a beautiful woman, but even with those legs of hers, she couldn't compete with twenty-something Brenna.

But I could call Lydia with my sympathy later. I couldn't believe Roger would think I was this desperate. "So I'm second choice."

"No." He sighed. "I knew you'd think that. Even when I was drunk, I wasn't fool enough to ask you, because it's not that really. I started thinking about what we had, and I missed you. Brenna only left me physically. I'd already left her emotionally."

I knew what he meant, because he'd left me emotionally a long, long time ago. We'd had a good marriage when the kids were little, but as he'd climbed higher in his firm, I wasn't enough. I suspected there were other women then--not that I could prove it. Then I'd taken this job, and he'd tried to come back and tell me what to do. It hadn't worked. And when he saw that it didn't work, he had the affair with Brenna--making it so flagrant, I couldn't ignore it.

I liked my life now. There was no one to control me. I felt pretty proud of the fact that I could support the kids. I couldn't go back. I wasn't even sure why I had put up with him for as long as I had. "Roger, I can't. I'm sorry."

"I want you to think about it," he said. "I don't want you to answer now. Just think about it. I know that this is a lot to absorb."

All I felt was pity for him. I didn't think my answer would change.

"So," in a deliberately more cheerful voice, he said, "What was it you called about?"

I laughed just a little. I had to, because I knew how it would sound. "I called to tell you that I was glad you weren't the arsonist."

"What? You didn't really think that I was, did you?"

"It crossed my mind after that last phone call."

"Because I said I wished that Beginnings had burned to the ground? Kaye, really."

"Well that, and the business with the Volvo still downtown the day after the fire."

"How did you know? But still--it doesn't make sense. I can't for a moment figure out why you ever thought that."

"So now that I know you didn't burn the safe house down, where were you that night?"

"You of all people must know I wasn't at your precious safe house."

"So?"

I heard a big sigh. "If you must know, Brenna has an apartment downtown. I spent the night, rode to work with her, and never even realized the car was on a snow route until I went to get it that night, and it was gone."

I believed him, if only because I could picture pretty well what happened when he couldn't find the car. From all I'd heard, parking in a snow emergency route resulted in one expensive ticket.

"So when did you realize that I wasn't the arsonist?" he asked.

"We caught him tonight."

"You caught him? You mean in the act?"

"Yup, he tried to set the place on fire again." I was enjoying this. After all, it wasn't like I could tell anybody else. Mo was gone. I hadn't even told my mother about the fire. I'd tell the kids that we'd caught the arsonist, but none of the details. I didn't want to worry them.

"Are you okay?"

"I'm fine. Everybody's fine. The safe house is fine." I deliberately made my voice sound bored. I didn't want to tell him how close I came to being toast--literally. I pushed the thought away; it could wait for a time when I felt ready to deal with it myself.

It suddenly occurred to me that my mother wasn't the only one I hadn't told about the fire. Roger and I hadn't exactly been best buds lately. "How come you know so much about this anyway?"

"I saw it on the news." He paused. "And I asked the kids to keep me updated, that okay?"

"Yeah, it's okay," I said softly.

"They said they heard you and Mo talking--and you thought it might be some minister."

"Yeah, you should have heard this guy. He was a real piece of work. And he was the first one at the hospital--which is what made us really wonder how he knew about it so fast."

"But it wasn't him, huh?"

"Nope, he just happened to be there visiting another parishioner when Mary Ellen came in."

He sighed again. "Anyway, Kaye, I'm glad it's over. The kids told me how hard this was on you. RJ said you knew your resident couldn't have committed suicide. It must feel good to know that you were right all along."

It did. Not because I'd wanted to be right particularly, but because it meant I hadn't misread my client so badly. I knew Mary Ellen hadn't committed suicide.

Actually, Pete Farrell wasn't half bad when I thought about it. Roger never would have admitted that I'd been right the way Farrell did. Farrell had a good body, too. He must work out. All that and blue eyes. "Roger, I've got to get off the phone now."

"Yes, I suppose you want to get to sleep, and I'd better get ready for work. Promise me you'll think about us, Kaye."

I didn't promise anything. It was just as well, since I hung up still thinking of Pete Farrell. But I was content to leave it at that. We hadn't made any definite plans but he'd call. If he didn't--well I had his work number. I'd use it, too. Some beginnings, like some endings, took a little work.

If you enjoyed this author's book, then please place a review up at the site of purchase, and any social media sites you frequent!

You can find ALL our books up on our website at:

https://www.writers-exchange.com

All Christine's Books:

https://www.writers-exchange.com/Christine-Duncan/

All our mysteries:

https://www.writers-exchange.com/category/genres/mystery-thrillers-suspense/

About the Author

Christine Duncan is the author of the Kaye Berreano mystery series. Safe House is the second book in the series. Christine resides in Colorado with her husband and children.

You can keep track of her books on her author page:

https://www.writers-exchange.com/Christine-Duncan/

If you want to read more about books by this author, they are listed on the following pages...

The Kaye Berreano Mystery Series

Battered women's shelter counsellor Kaye Berreano searches out the complexities of minds and hearts...along with solving the seemingly never-ending mysteries that keep cropping up around her.

Book 1: Safe Beginnings

When the fire alarm at a battered women's shelter goes off, counselor Kaye Berreano rushes to evacuate the residents, but she's too late. Her patient Mary Ellen is dead. Farrell, the skeptical arson investigator, believes Kaye knows who set the fire.

Farrell's main theory is that Mary Ellen, in a moment of suicidal crisis, set the fire herself. Kaye knows Mary Ellen was *not* suicidal.

Kaye launches her own investigation while dealing with Farrell, attending to her divorce and caring for two teenagers. From a roommate who fought with Mary Ellen, to another patient at the shelter who's in the safe house mistakenly by court order, to a fanatical minister from Mary Ellen's church who doesn't believe in divorce for any reason, Kaye discovers suspects and motives aplenty...while the truth remains just out of reach.

Publisher: https://www.writers-exchange.com/safe-beginnings/

Book 2: Safe House

With snow falling and Thanksgiving coming up fast, Colorado is plunged into a winter wonderland. Battered women's counselor Kaye Berreano doesn't have time to celebrate. She has two teens at home that tend to claim most of her attention along with a new relationship with police investigator Pete Farrell. Already feeling overwhelmed, Kaye isn't sure she can take much more when a kid she's known since birth turns up dead and her own son RJ becomes a suspect. Forced into an investigation, she's led from the safe house...to her own house.

Publisher: https://www.writers-exchange.com/safe-house/